ADMIRAL OF ENGLAND

Admiral of England

by

SHOWELL STYLES

Faber and Faber
London

*First published in 1973
by Faber and Faber Limited
3 Queen Square London WC1
Printed in Great Britain by
Latimer Trend & Company Ltd Plymouth
All rights reserved*

ISBN 0 571 10428 2

AUTHOR'S NOTE

It may add to the interest of this book to know that all its chief characters really existed and that all the main incidents actually happened.

PROLOGUE

Morning was a grey glimmer in the mist when the woman came hurrying down through the rocks to the beach. It was still too dark to see colours. The huge waves that rolled into Porth Hellick cove looked almost black; the white sand of Scilly, like snow when the sun dazzled on it, was like ashes now compared to the flash of the bursting spray. There were specks and streaks of black farther along the ashen ribbon of sand, midway between the retreating surf and the granite rocks above the cove. The woman made along the beach towards them, her head thrust forward like the muzzle of a coursing hound. The sea-wind whipped her skirts about her bare striding ankles and set her long hair streaming as stiff and straight as the whip at the masthead of a King's ship.

Beyond the incessant thunder of the breaking waves, in the interval between their roars of self-destruction, she could hear another sound, something between a growl and a snarl. Everyone on St Mary's knew that sound. It was the voice of the Gilstone. They had a saying in Hugh Town that you could hear the Gilstone growling like a dog with a bone when it had done the business of yet another great ship; and last night—Long Ben had said it, and he was seldom wrong—three great ships had gone to splinters on the Gilstone ledges. Others had heard the crash of breaking masts and some swore to hearing shrieks. Their eyes had glistened as they told of it, running from cottage to cottage to spread the news. For all were good neighbours on St Mary's, and a wreck meant pickings for all according to what he or she could find. The woman frowned as she stumbled hastily along the line of weed that marked high water. All Hugh Town, except herself, had gone running to the strand where Long Ben predicted the bodies would come ashore. But for the remembered words of her dead father she would have gone with them.

"Porth Hellick's the place, my wench," he had told her. "If they get a boat away and make any distance before she overturns as she must, the drift will bring 'em into Porth Hellick. And—mark me—them in the boat will be officers and gentry."

There had never been an Islander who knew more about wrecks—and wrecking too. But this was to stake all on a cast of ambs-ace. If there had been no time for launching of boats, if the three great ships had gone to pieces on the Gilstone and sent all their broken remnant drifting to the other beaches, then she would miss her fair share of the harvest God had appointed for Scilly from the beginning of seafaring. A thousand, maybe two thousand bodies to come ashore in His good time. Money, clothes, lords and captains with gold about them and jewelled sword-hilts. The woman muttered a prayer, soliciting at least a little of that bounty to reward her faith.

A hundred paces ahead a thin black line crossed the irregular bank of wrack. An oar. It was a sign, an answer to her prayer. A few yards beyond it she came upon a small naked body that she took at first for the corpse of a child. It was a dead dog, a little hairless greyhound. But the dark figure prone on the sand farther on was no dog, and she ran to it, nearly falling in her haste.

A big man and stout. It took most of her wiry strength to turn him over, to come at what was under the sodden coat that lay across his head and upper body. The growing light showed her a heavy-jowled face with closed eyes, a skull short-cropped and wigless; but her hungry glance passed at once to the hands. Her efforts had left the arms lying across his chest (a coat heavy with gold braid, she discerned with a gasp of excitement) and on each of the hands there was a large ring.

The one on the right hand bore an enormous jewel—an emerald, she thought. The clammy flesh woke no revulsion in her as she knelt quickly and seized the hand with the emerald ring. More quickly still she let it fall and shrank back on her haunches. It had moved in her grasp. At the same instant the big man had let out a groan, slight indeed and scarcely audible above the thunder of the surf but enough to prove the life still in him.

The woman half raised her clenched fist as if to shake it at the heavens. Unjust! To throw ambs-ace and then be denied her winnings! This was some great man, an admiral perhaps, and she dared not take the rings if he was to live. And yet God had answered her prayer—God could not mean her to refuse His gift. Faith, the minister had said, was of little worth without Works.

The big man groaned faintly, once more, as she bent over him again.

ONE

The boy Clow sat with his arms hugging the smooth timber of *Victory*'s foretopmast and his legs swinging to the rise and scend of her racing hull far below him. His round face bore a scowl of intense concentration. His gaze was fixed on the long dun-coloured cloud of smoke that hid the northern horizon, lying across the flat grey-green expanse of sea. To larboard and starboard of *Victory* raced the other twenty-three great ships of Prince Rupert's squadron under full sail, a sight to set a landsman agape with admiration, but at 16 Clow Shovell was as familiar with great ships as a London lad would be with noblemen's coaches. It was the Dutch ships he was looking for, and they were somewhere in that dun-coloured cloud pounding away at King Charles's General-at-Sea and his diminished fleet.

The brisk westerly, cold for an evening in early June, had chilled his body in its linen shirt and drawers but he was unconscious of it. The chill took physical effect upon him, all the same. On deck he would have gone to the lee scuppers to relieve himself, but up here he had to manage as best he could, contriving like a good seaman to send the wind-driven spray of urine to leeward. The necessity did him a service by forcing his gaze away from the battle-cloud. As he readjusted his clothes and position he glanced to windward and saw what he ought to have seen a minute or two earlier—the low dark loom of the land.

"De-e-eck! Deck, there! Sou' Foreland abeam to larboard!"

Down at the foot of the foremast one of the hands waved an

acknowledgement of his hail and trotted aft to report. Clow
shook his tow-coloured mop of hair in self-admonishment; he
had nearly earned a clout from the shipmaster, or—worse still
—a word of reproof from Sir Christopher. But he could not
keep his eyes from the smoke-cloud ahead. Five minutes ago
the frigate in advance of the squadron had let fly her topgallant
sheets and fired a gun, in token that she had sighted the enemy,
before vanishing at once into the smoke. A continuous thunder
was in his ears already, rising above the deafening rush of the
wind—the guns. Hundreds and hundreds of guns. De Ruyter
(he had heard Mr Narbrough say it) had more than a hundred
ships and that meant five or six thousand guns on the Dutch
side alone. If you added the Duke's—but here came a black
speck out of the smoke-cloud, and another. Two ships, or hulls
that had once been ships. Masts gone from both, one of them
with a plume of black smoke drifting aslant from her deck. The
thunder of battle was much louder now. Clow Shovell was
phlegmatic, as a Norfolk man should be; indeed, he displayed
already a singular composure, curiously like that of *Victory's*
first lieutenant, John Narbrough. But despite his resolution
to remain unmoved by every circumstance of sea-life his heart
thumped to the loudening thunder of the guns.

"Clow, bor! Shift-ho—room for yer elders an' betters!"

Dick Parr's leathery face grinned up at him from the level
of his dangling bare feet. Dick was swinging precariously with
one hand on the ratlines and a foot braced against the mast.
Like Clow, he was from Cockthorpe.

"Cap'n Chris'm wantin' his lady's-maid," he added, wink-
ing.

Clow's rating as ship's boy did not prevent his employment
as personal attendant to Sir Christopher Myngs, a neighbour
at Cockthorpe and with Clowdisley blood in him. The wit of
the waisters and fo'c's'le hands on this theme had long ceased
to bother Clow.

"Then I'll draw down, bor," he returned, and swung off

his perch to cling to the upper ratlines while Parr took his place.

The dizzy backwards climb down the sagging rope rungs to the deck was a thrice-daily exercise and hardly to be noticed in the few seconds it took him. Scarcely had he sprung from the bulwarks to the planking when the startling uproar of the drums surged through the ship and he was engulfed in a great swarm of men running from all directions to get to their battle quarters, shouting and jesting in broad Norfolk as they ran. Clow, fighting his way towards the poop, hated the muddle and noise; he always had done and he always would. In a King's ship, to his way of thinking, orders should be obeyed in silence, and instead of this undisciplined rabble in dirty jerkins and drawers of every hue there should be seamen uniformly dressed and rigidly drilled.

He won through to the clearer space abaft the mainmast and up the three steps to the quarter-deck. Sir Christopher and the first lieutenant were standing together at the carved rail, peering ahead under the arching canvas of the mainsail. There was no crucifix on *Victory*'s quarter-deck (Myngs, who had served under Blake, was no Papist) but Clow knuckled his forehead as he came up the broad wooden steps. What with the crews of the quarter-deck cannon, the two seamen at the helm, the master and his mate, and half a dozen musketeers on the poop ramming and priming in a group round the mizzen-mast, the after-deck was unusually crowded. Above the gilded stern-lantern the huge red ensign flapped and snapped; Sir Christopher was vice-admiral of the Red in this joint command of a Bohemian prince and a one-time general of Cromwell's army. Clow stood stiffly behind the two officers. It was not for him to interrupt their discourse.

"I fear the Prince will be half mad with fury," Narbrough was saying deprecatingly.

"Wholly mad, Mr Narbrough. Rupert's half mad to begin with." Sir Christopher's big voice was jovial. "But small wonder, sir, when he's sent to chase a French fleet that's not there, while the mynheers seize their chance and set upon Albemarle."

"God send we come in time," said Narbrough, but without emotion.

His neat figure in a suit of sober grey was in contrast with his superior officer, whose large frame was clad in a long and much-stained buff coat that sorted ill with purple breeches and silver-buckled shoes. With his ruddy cheeks and long curling hair Myngs looked like a Cavalier of thirty years ago; whereas he had no love for the Stuarts, boasted that his father was a shoemaker and his mother a hoyman's daughter, and had held his knighthood only since the Solebay sea-fight last year. Turning now and espying the waiting boy, he gave him a nod and a smile.

"To my cabin, Clow. Back and breast, sword and baldric. And at speed, for we'll be into 'em in the twinkle of an eye— that's the Prince's trumpet."

The thin high note was in Clow's ears as he leaped from the quarter-deck, and a quick glance showed him the red flag hanging in the mizzen shrouds of a ship far out on the starboard beam. The squeal of the trumpet made the growing noise of gunfire seem like the roll of giant drums. A hoarse voice came from nearer at hand.

"Gunners! Load your pieces!"

The racket of heavy stamping and the rumbling of wooden trucks drowned all other noises when Clow was inside Sir Christopher's cabin. John Clowdisley, secretary to the vice-admiral, was there writing at a table. Clowdisley was a Blakeney man and Clow's second cousin.

"From this devil's dance overhead," he said in his acid tones, "I take it we are about to engage the Dutch."

"Yis, Mr Clowdisley." Clow, who was at a closet in the bulkhead loading himself with gear, spoke without turning. "Be you drawin' on deck to see?"

"When the hurly-burly's done. When the battle's lost and won," returned the secretary, flourishing his quill. "Yours to fight, mine to write, Cousin Clow."

Clow clattered out and up the ladder, and the acrid smell of burnt powder was in his nostrils. *Victory*, in the van of Prince Rupert's squadron, was entering the smoke-cloud. Aloft on fore and main the hands were taking in the topgallant sails while others swarmed on the bowsprit lowering spritsail and sprit-topsail. Clow, who had sailed a boat since he was old enough to climb into one, told himself that in the Prince's place he would have had his squadron take in main courses also, for greater ease of manœuvring. But this was no time for nautical theorizing.

Narbrough had gone for'ard to his battle-station. Sir Christopher, who had mounted to the poop-deck, was giving orders to Frisby, the chief gunner, and continued to do so while Clow settled the steel back and breast round his upper body and slung the sword to his shoulder by its embroidered baldric.

"Hold your hand while we're in smoke, Mr Frisby. When you shoot, be sure it's at your enemy." His naturally loud voice was raised to a shout to overtop the din of gunfire from ships still invisible. "Half gunshot before you fire. Remember that and see that your gun-crews remember it. Now begone."

Frisby touched a finger to his flat cap and scuttled away down the ladder. Sir Christopher wriggled his broad shoulders under the body-armour and patted his sword-hilt.

"Clow, you'll stay by me to carry messages." His eye fell on the boy's resolutely expressionless face and he grinned, not unkindly, recalling that this was young Clowdisley Shovell's first sea-fight. "No need to look like a parson that's wet his breeches, lad. It's a game—we stake our bodies but it's a game. You'll find——"

A series of shattering explosions cut him short. The ship on their larboard side had opened fire. A second later a tall dark shape grew out of the drifting smoke ahead, with a second shape beyond it. Myngs ran to the lee rail to peer at them.

"Hogen Mogen, both of 'em!" he roared joyfully. "Shipmaster, take me between those Dutchmen!"

Victory under main and topsails was still surging ahead at speed. The great brown hulls of the enemy vessels seemed to hurtle towards her, their upper decks black with men and their shot-torn sails flapping. Clow stood gripping the taffrail and gulping convulsively, aware of mingled terror and excitement yet more keenly aware of small details—the perspective of smoking matches where the crews stood by *Victory*'s upper-deck guns, the shuffle of the musketeers taking their stations by the rail, a sudden rift in the smoke to starboard that gave a glimpse of a dozen or more great ships with their guns belching smoke, the vermilion curlicues on the carved Dutch beakhead that came sliding towards them. Then all was swept away in a vast outburst of noise that stunned and deafened him, a billowing cloud of smoke that hid all but a few yards of the after-deck below him. Into that clear patch fell a man's body, to lie twitching in a spreading red pool. It had no head. *Victory* was jerking and shuddering as the balls thudded into her side, and the body's limbs moved as if it was still alive. Clow dragged his gaze away to glance at Sir Christopher, who raised an arm to point above them. A masthead with an orange-barred flag trailing from it slid past as if suspended above the smoke, tilting as it went and finally tumbling out of sight.

"Mizzen!" crowed Myngs, and turned to shout to the deck. "Well done, starboard guns!"

They could hear him because the firing had ceased except for the ceaseless din of more distant guns. It was a moment or two before Clow's dulled hearing could discern the thin high chorus of cries and moans from *Victory*'s gun decks, and Frisby's yell topped it almost at once.

"Blow your matches, larboard side!"

The second Dutch ship loomed alongside and vanished in another eruption of smoke and flame and noise. Despite himself Clow shut his eyes and gripped the taffrail as if his life depended on the strength of his fingers, staying thus until his eardrums were no longer assailed by the stupefying din. When he could look about him again there was a long white splinter standing up from the wooden rail a foot from his fingers and a ragged gap in the poop bulwarks four paces away. Two of the musketeers were dead; the master's mate, having lugged them out of the way, was wiping his hands on the seat of his breeches and gazing astern at the rapidly diminishing Dutch vessel. The smoke of the two broadsides was shredding away before a stiffening breeze and it could be seen that the Dutchman had only one mast standing and was listing heavily; damage, as Clow realized, gained in an earlier fight. Two more ships swam out of the haze, both on the larboard side and both enveloped in their own haze of gun-smoke. The nearer ship wore the Dutch colours and *Victory* discharged her broadside at her as she surged past. Clearly the Prince intended to take the squadron through without pausing to engage.

Clow had learned from fo'c's'le gossip that the fight between Albemarle's fifty-six ships and De Ruyter's eighty-five was now in its third day, having begun off Dungeness on the last day of May; a spritsail barge out of Solent had given that news. So there could be few vessels, save the inevitable proportion of deserters, that had not been under close fire. John Clowdisley had him told how the King's General-at-Sea, giving credence to a rumour that the French had sailed from Brest, had hastily detached Prince Rupert (unwillingly his junior in command) with twenty-four ships to intercept the French fleet and prevent its junction with the Dutch. To Clow this had seemed incredibly foolish, a silly flinging away of the opportunity to deal with De Ruyter first and the less formidable ships of King Louis later, and he had said so, provoking the secretary to sarcasm.

"You, Master Shovell, are merely a seaman familiar with the sea. His Grace of Albemarle—General Monk to the vulgar —is a great man familiar with His Majesty. He may choose, as he did last year, to sail his fleet across the Goodwins and run twelve ships aground and still be right."

The Goodwins were in Clow's mind as, with senses reviving after that last broadside, he looked round him for Sir Christopher, for he knew the course of the squadron must have brought them off the Downs by now. Sir Christopher could be seen only as an expanse of purple breeches. He was hanging head downwards across the larboard rail, and for a moment the boy thought he was dead or wounded; until he righted himself briskly and turned to address his messenger.

"My service to Mr Narbrough and I'll have the carpenter's party to inspect the after-hold. Tell him we may be holed on the water-line. Off with you!"

Clow knuckled his forehead and sprang to obey. But he darted an apprehensive glance ahead from the top of the poop ladder. They were out of the smoke and there was open sea ahead, grey under the evening overcast and dotted with the white sails of a dozen ships too far away to be identifiable; no more fighting, then—yet. Avoiding the blackened, loudly jesting men round the after guns, he made his way along the planked gangway that linked the after-deck to the fore-deck, with the open ports of the starboard lower-deck guns down on his right above the racing waves and the crowded waist below on his left. The waist was a turmoil of noise and stink that sickened him. There were dead men there and others half alive; men shrieking as they were carried down to the orlop to endure the crudest of surgery; men drinking from leather jacks, men stoically binding splinter wounds with dirty rags. It was a relief to find the first lieutenant by the foremast-foot superintending the splicing of a parted stay. Narbrough had the carpenter and his men on their way aft in a matter of seconds; Clow followed them as far as the after hatchway and so up to the quarter-deck, where he found Sir Christopher with a perspective glass to his eye gazing south-westward.

"God's life!" swore Sir Christopher, and oaths were rare in his mouth; he spoke to the master, who stood beside him. "It's *Royal Prince*, aground on the Galloper and Dutch colours at the main. Ayscue's struck—I'd never credit that if I'd not seen it."

Clow, looking with them, had his first clear sight of the warring fleets.

The wind, veering a little northerly, had swept the gun-smoke into a long dun-coloured barrier some two miles astern of *Victory*. Dull orange flashes from within the barrier showed that fighting was going on there, with a considerable number of vessels engaged; but even so the intervening sea seemed crowded with ships. Beyond the nearer sails of Rupert's ships, the rearmost of which were firing as they came through the fringe of the battle, the grey waters were speckled with brown and black and red hulls—with wreckage, too, of great ships burnt or torn apart. Some were in groups of three or two or four, half hidden in the smoke of conflict; others manœuvred slowly in line against an opposing line of enemy vessels. More numerous were the single ships, dismasted and motionless or drifting under improvised sails, many with boats moving about them. But what took and held the eye was a very great ship towards the landward side of the battle, unmoving and with her masts aslant, her sails hanging in rags from the spars. The Dutch flag floated from the mainmast of Sir George Ayscue's *Royal Prince*, aground on the Galloper Sand; and seemingly the Dutch proposed to make prize of her. Boats were plying back and forth from a trio of Dutchmen anchored well to leeward of her and Clow thought they were passing a cable. Four ships of Rupert's squadron were turning to spoil their plan, though.

"They've fired her, damn them!" exclaimed Sir Christopher furiously; and indeed a thin column of black smoke was rising between the tilted masts. "Fired *Royal Prince*, that was Blake's flagship *Resolution* when I served——"

21

"Admiral's going about, sir." The master interrupted him without ceremony and sprang away to bellow down at the deck. "Hands to the braces!"

The flagship, far out on their windward side with the red flag that meant *Engage the enemy* trailing from her mizzen shrouds, was turning into the wind. Within a minute each of the other twenty-three ships had done the same. The completion of the turn brought the wind a trifle abaft the beam, and with the strengthening breeze at their best point of sailing the squadron, spread irregularly across the whole battle area, bore swiftly down on the enemy.

II

"It's Rupert's *métier*, of course—the charge," said John Clowdisley. "It served the purpose today. Tomorrow we shall need somewhat more than cavalry tactics."

He was sitting on a low stool beside the bunk in his tiny box of a cabin, where a candle threw strange shadows across his saturnine features. Clow Shovell lay in the bunk and his second cousin was removing clotted blood from a long gash in his forearm with the aid of a cloth and a bowl of salt water. *Victory* was at anchor in the Downs, with the rest of the English fleet, and the time was a little before midnight.

"He said well who first announced that blood is thicker than water," Clowdisley added drily, using the cloth.

He was point-device in black velvet and silvered lace, for he had not long returned from attending Sir Christopher to the conference on board the Lord High Admiral's ship. That the proverb he quoted in jest had real meaning for him was proved by the secretary's actions on his return. *Victory* was still a dark muddle of broken timber and tangled cordage, where parties wrought haphazardly by lantern-light to remedy the battle-damage and the dead lay in black bundles along the scuppers. Clowdisley had sought his kinsman among the chaos and found him at last in the cockpit with threescore of wounded and dying men; he had been dragged there after being knocked senseless by a falling spar in the last minutes of the fight. The secretary had conveyed him to his own cabin and there applied such rudiments of surgery as he possessed, which included the letting of blood and application of hot poultices, with the result that the boy had regained consciousness. It was perhaps not very strange that after losing a deal of blood from the cut in his arm, and a further half-pint by Clowdisley's surgery, he should be feeling too weak to move. Recollection of the events before he had been felled by the spar was returning slowly, but he realized that the fighting had been broken off at nightfall as was customary and that the hammering and banging that resounded through the ship were the noise of repair work in progress.

"A clean bandage and six hours' sleep." Clowdisley was still patiently sponging away the dried blood. "These, Clowdisley Shovell of Cockthorpe, will fit you for tomorrow's engagement."

Clow winced as the pain of the flesh wound overcame the throbbing pain in his head. "We fight tomorrow, then?"

"So it is resolved by our lords and masters—in order to save, I take it, our credit as sea-fighters. I believe the Duke of York would have saved his ships and let the credit go, though our Jamie is no coward. But the soldiers—God bless them and give them sense—over-persuaded him."

While he finished the sponging and prepared to apply a linen bandage the secretary talked on, his dry incisive tones sketching the scene in the great cabin of the *Royal James*. There had been Sir Christopher and his fellow vice-admirals Sir Thomas Allen and Sir Edward Spragge, Prince Rupert in his favourite scarlet and silver, the Duke of Albemarle who seemed a gross and ageing caricature of that General Monck who had been Cromwell's right hand. Presiding over this Council of War was the King's brother, James Duke of York and Lord High Admiral, dark-featured and unprepossessing, obstinate and yet easily swayed by stronger personalities. At

23

a side table the secretaries sat with their quills and tablets. Since the Dutch had had the best of it, the conference began with angry words and attempts to apportion the blame for failure, Rupert accusing Albemarle of insensate folly in dispatching him on a wild-goose chase and Albemarle accusing the Prince of dilatoriness in rejoining the fleet. James had overborne this quarrel by asserting roundly that his admirals had utterly failed to control their captains; in which there was some truth, for at least nine of those captains, tiring of the battle, had chosen to desert it while their vessels were still intact and were now safe in port. Next the vice-admirals spoke up in their own defence, declaring that at bottom the Navy Board was to blame. Their ships were ill-found and old, half their crews were pressed landsmen, there had been no pay for seamen since before the Plague; if they wanted persistence against hard fighters like the Dutch this state of things would have to be remedied and at once. This had led to long and futile argument about matters impertinent to the present battle, while the secretaries' quills were idle for an hour by the clock.

Clow heard the tale with one half of his dulled consciousness. The other half was engaged in recollection of the last two hours of that day's fighting. For him it had the quality of a nightmare, a Bedlam. Twice more had Prince Rupert led his squadron—or its dwindling nucleus—clean through the crowded battle area, never bringing-to to engage but dealing such damage as he could with passing broadsides. That his ships received as good as they gave or better was likely enough; *Victory* had lost one-third of her crew of 530, by death or by wounds that were death's equivalent in those hopeless circumstances. And nothing had been achieved save the proof that men like Christopher Myngs and John Narbrough could remain sane in Bedlam. Clow, dodging back and forth with messages through the increasing chaos of wreckage and slaughter on the decks, knew little of what was going on outside his own ship. From Sir Christopher's utterances he deduced that the vice-admiral was in much the same case. When in the deepening twilight they drew clear after the final onslaught *Victory* was one of the four vessels of the squadron to hold in company with the Prince's flagship; the rest had either borne away from the fight or steered for some part of the battle where they might have a chance of prize or booty, some of them with mutinous crews who had superseded their incompetent captains. There had been mutiny even in *Victory*, where most of the seamen were Norfolk men who loved their captain like a father; a score of landsmen, pressed from Holme and Brancaster at the outset, had barricaded themselves in the hold and stayed there through all the fighting. It was all a part of the general muddle that pervaded the fleet of His Majesty King Charles the Second, and Clow Shovell hated it because he had a certain dim vision of a Navy disciplined and supreme.

One thing had surprised Clow in those confused hours of intermittent battle: his own reaction to the grim sights and sounds of the brief engagements. The thing that most revolted his orderly mind was the mess and confusion that grew all round him. The fear of death no longer troubled him, nor the sight of blood and mangled bodies. If he felt some apprehension at the thought of more sea-fighting tomorrow, it was chiefly a fear that this acquired indifference would not stay with him. Perhaps, he thought, shifting bruised limbs painfully on the hard palliasse, he had now passed his apprenticeship, just as a butcher had to pass his.

"And so the upshot of it all was a resolution which we secretaries solemnly noted down." John Clowdisley finished his bandaging with a neat tie. "To wit, that this fleet shall set upon the enemy next morning. I doubt there'll be some who will set upon a course for the nearest harbour so soon as the admirals are occupied with fighting."

"Why can't all obey?" asked Clow, flexing his wounded arm and grunting as it stung. "The seamen to the captains and the captains to the admirals?"

25

Clowdisley had stooped to grope in a locker below the bunk. Now he stood up with a bottle and a large glass in his hands and filled a bumper.

"The seamen will obey when they've a seaman to command them," he said. "Your spriggish gallants and dashing country squires, that command—or can't command—half our ships, are babes playing with fire when they take to the sea, and the men know it. As for the captains, there's a few like our own that will strive to pull the fat out of the fire for the admirals. And as for the admirals—why, God bless you, His Majesty and the Navy Board make them out of whatever materials they have to hand." He placed the brimming glass in Clow's free hand. "It's ripe Madeira. You'll sleep after it."

The yellow candlelight woke a warm red glow in the wine, and as it vanished down Clow's throat it woke the same glow in his body. He returned the empty glass and lay back.

"I will take a glass myself," said Clowdisley, doing so. "Wine at a proper time is good, saith Ovidius Naso, and when a man is weary as I am, then is a proper time. Does your arm pain you greatly?"

There was no reply. Clow was asleep. The secretary nodded satisfaction and finished his wine. Then he took an old furred gown from a hook, pinched out the candle, and having wrapped himself in the gown lay down on the deck to sleep.

III

For three days the bodies had been coming ashore on the strands between Ramsgate and St Margaret's. The next day was to see the end of the Four Days' Battle. By noon of that day, June 3rd, the unceasing thunder-roll sounding out of the eastward haze told the Kentish longshoremen that there would be more of the grisly harvest to be reaped.

The wind had backed in the night and fallen away to light airs, so that although the English anchors were a-cockbill at daybreak the morning was well advanced before the rear of the fleet had weathered the tip of the Goodwins. Nor was it the lack of wind alone that slowed the progress of Albemarle's ships. Not one of them but hoisted sails full of shot-holes and great rents, and the masts of some carried curious arrangements of canvas that told of spars destroyed by the Dutch balls. For this was the loyal remnant of the eighty ships that had sailed from the Nore, forty-nine battered and patched-up vessels depleted in crews and weakened in fire-power but resolute to fight it out to the end. Of the rest, nineteen were sunk or captured by the Dutch; the others had run.

Victory led the van this day, and proudly. Myngs was a seaman born and bred and the Norfolk men he commanded had done their best for love of him. The worst of the damage to her sails had been roughly codged over, the gaps in her rail fenced with hawser, and the broken mizzen topsail yard—the same that had nearly cracked Clow Shovell's skull in its fall—fished with a jury spar which Sir Christopher had prudently brought with him from Chatham. Five of her eighty-two guns were now incapable of firing (which, as Dick Parr pointed out to Clow, made her a third-rate instead of a second-rate), but since she had barely enough hands left for the manning of seventy guns this made no difference to her state. Among the Red squadron that followed her was one of the two sixth-raters that had been converted into fireships by cramming them with combustibles and supplying them with one ship's boat and a minimum crew; having grappled their craft to a Dutchman and ignited her, the men would abandon ship and pull clear. It was said in the forecastle that Sir Christopher planned to avenge the burning of Sir George Ayscue's ship, whose gutted carcase still lay smoking on the Goodwins.

With the change of wind had come a change of weather. The day was sunless but warm, with hardly breeze enough to raise furrows on the long oily swell. The Dutch ships were keeping well to eastward of the Sands and the thick haze prevented the English van from sighting them until the two fleets were less than a mile apart, when De Ruyter's ships were seen to be ranged in a long irregular line and moving slowly northward, with the flagship near their centre. With drums beating to quarters and her torn red ensign flapping slowly as she altered course, *Victory* bore down on the Dutch flagship.

Long afterwards John Narbrough told Clow that this day's encounter was like the end of a fist-fight he had once seen at Lynn fair, when two weary men smashed on at each other though each could scarce raise an arm to defend himself. The Dutch losses in ships and men had been little more than a quarter of the English; but the ships in their line of battle on the fourth day had received so fierce a battering that they could not deal Albemarle's diminished fleet the punishment it invited. *Victory*, fighting yard-arm to yard-arm with *Eendracht*, could hold her own and more against De Ruyter's tired gunners, who had fought for three successive days. At the end of an hour both ships had lost their mizzen-masts and their decks were heaped with smashed timber and cordage and mutilated bodies. But the guns crashed on and on. And in the midst of the tumult Clow Shovell was happy.

Back and forth went Clow through the din and the smoke, sole means of communication between the poop and foredeck of the reeling, shuddering *Victory*. Each time he made the journey the confusion and horror of the upper deck were worse; but because this bedlam was a by-product of purposeful efficiency he could tolerate it. Sir Christopher's purpose had been made known throughout the ship before she left the Downs. The biggest single blow that could be struck at the enemy was the capture or destruction of Admiral De Ruyter's flagship, which (it was said) carried no less a person than the Grand Pensionary of the United Netherlands. For all her inferior force, *Victory* was as capable of striking that blow as any first-rate in Albemarle's command, for her seamen and gunners knew their crafts and her officers knew their ship. Disdaining reply to the cannonade that greeted *Victory* as she drove through the outer line of Dutchmen, Myngs with superb seamanship had taken her straight alongside the 76-gun *Eendracht*. Now it was for the gunners to show themselves better men than the Dutch who outnumbered them by nearly two to one. And they were doing it. Their fire was more rapid and more accurate, especially from the for'ard guns where John Narbrough, a reddened bandage round his head, walked coolly from one sweating gun-crew to the next, steadying the excited gunners and occasionally pointing a gun himself. It was Narbrough who by concentrating the fire of his guns succeeded at last in bringing down De Ruyter's mainmast.

The rending crash of the great spar was a startling noise even amid the thunder of gunfire. For a moment Clow thought the powder magazine in one or other of the ships had blown up—an ever-present fear with fighting seamen at times like this. Reassured, he struggled aft with Narbrough's reply to the message he had borne from Sir Christopher, which had asked for reinforcements to be sent to help the party of landsmen trying to cut away the wreckage of the mizzen-mast. He watched the vice-admiral's face with anxiety as he reported that reply.

"Mr Narbrough's service, sir, and he can send no men without detaching from the gun-crews and so awaits a further order. And, sir—Mr Narbrough bade me ask, what of the fire-ship?"

Sir Christopher's body-armour showed a dent in the breast where a musket-ball had been turned and his buff coat was spattered with blood. He had his drawn sword in his hand—he was on the poop directing the fire of the musketeers—and as he turned to Clow with his blue eyes ablaze and his long hair flying he presented a wild figure.

"What of the fireship!" he repeated, bellowing against the uproar. "Ask it of that devil's spawn Phillips! Yonder he lies—you may see the rogue's topsails—'stead of laying alongside as he was bid!"

His hand shook with fury as he pointed with the sword-blade

to a gap in the swirling smoke. Clow had almost forgotten that other ships beside his own were engaged in close combat. Now, peering through the smoke and beyond *Eendracht*'s gilded beakhead, he glimpsed a jumble of tattered sails and flame-spouting hulls at the farther end of an alley of clear water. The fireship *Arabella* lay idle under backed topsails in that patch of sea.

"The poxy fool! Why a'God's name does he wait?" Sir Christopher was beside himself with rage. "He has the wind-ward—if he'd but bring his flames to the Dutchman's other beam De Ruyter must strike to us. My sword to the knave's rump! Would I might win to him and lay it there!"

"I could——" Clow paused and gulped. "I could swim to her with your orders, Sir Christopher."

The smoke had closed the gap but he had gauged the distance. A cable's length—nothing to a Cockthorpe lad who swam as easily as he walked. It was only sudden remembrance of his wounded arm that had made him hesitate.

Sir Christopher was staring at him open-mouthed. Now he clapped him on the shoulder and spoke rapidly.

"The stern gallery—jacob's-ladder coiled at the rail, larboard side. Tell Captain Phillips——"

His voice ceased in a choked cry and he clapped a hand to his throat. Blood rushed out between his fingers. Clow sprang forward but was waved back by Sir Christopher's free hand holding the sword.

"Go!" the vice-admiral mouthed at him; and Clow went at a run.

Down from the poop to the half-deck and through into the great stern cabin. Out of the door on to the low-beamed gallery overhanging the dingy waves. The jacob's-ladder uncoiled as he flung it down from the carved oaken rail and he clambered back-downwards on its sagging hemp rungs until he felt the chill water at his hams and let go with an awkward plunge.

With the first stroke he thought the gash in his forearm had opened. The sting of the salt pained for a few seconds and then passed, leaving a freedom of movement he hadn't expected; this circumstance, and the feel of cold water after the sweat and smoke of the fight, gave him confidence and even exhilaration. After a first detour to get round the mizzenmast rigging, which trailed astern over *Victory*'s quarter, he swam straight under the Dutch flagship's bows and struck out for the *Arabella* with rather less than two hundred yards to go. It crossed his mind that the Dutch musketeers might see him and open fire, but so far as he could tell in the general din of firing no musket-shot was aimed at him. Painful collision with a fragment of timber warned him to watch his course as he toiled over the long smooth swell. A biscuit's-toss to his left a man holding on to a broken spar cried piteously to him in Dutch, but he shut his ears to the cry and quickened his stroke.

The fireship's side rose above him and he trod water, shouting at the untenanted rail overhead that he was from *Victory* with admiral's orders. Minutes passed before a rope's end splashed beside him. Clow could climb a rope with any man, but the action pained his arm far more than the movement of swimming and but for the knots at half-fathom intervals he would never have reached the rail. He was hauled over and found himself confronted by half a dozen men who eyed him sullenly.

"I've to—speak with Captain Phillips," he said, getting his breath.

"I'm Captain Phillips." A squat, beetle-browed man stepped forward. "Give me your dispatch."

"I carry none, sir. Vice-Admiral Myngs bids you close at once, light your fires, and——"

"I'll take no orders from your mouth, my lad," Phillips snapped. "Let Sir Christopher send in proper form and maybe I'll move."

"But, sir——"

"Look yonder." Phillips pointed to the great hull half

buried in flame-shot smoke, one mast only left standing with its torn shreds of sail. "She's done. Myngs can finish her without my aid." He turned to scowl at Clow, who was standing tense and incredulous with the blood from his wound dripping into the pool of water at his feet. "You'd better get below and tend your hurt."

"You won't go?" Clow demanded between clenched teeth; there was no *sir* this time.

Phillips glanced at his men and then glared at Clow.

"I stay," he shouted angrily. "And so—do *you*!"

Clow dodged his clawing grasp by an inch, spun on his heel and was over the rail in a single headlong leap. The water closed above his head. When he broke surface he made only a few strokes before duck-diving and continuing underwater for as long as his breath lasted; he could not be sure in the noise that was all around him, but he thought a pistol had been fired at him from *Arabella*'s rail. The anger that rose in him, that made him forget the stab of pain each time he made an armstroke, was not at the pistol-shot. He raged inwardly that Phillips could not be brought to book for his disobedience. Apart from the fact that the man (as John Clowdisley had told him) had procured his captaincy through the favour of the Duke of Buckingham, there was the traditional licence of a ship's captain to do as he thought best with his ship. Fool or coward, Phillips had in all likelihood prevented the final destruction of the Dutch flagship—and he would suffer no penalty. While such a thing was possible, Clow told himself wrathfully, there would always be muddle in His Majesty's fleets. Vaguely at the back of his mind was the vision of a Navy ruled by a rigid discipline and, through that discipline, ruler of the seas.

The inferno of smoke and flame and noise grew fiercer as he swam unseen beneath *Eendracht*'s beakhead. A sight of *Victory*'s poop filled him with dismay. A great splintered gap yawned below her rail where the side windows of the stern cabin had been and wisps of black smoke curled from its edges. Men could be discerned busy at the rail and on the stern gallery with water-buckets. Clow swam the faster for his jacob's-ladder, thankful that it hung from the larboard end of the gallery; the starboard end had vanished, part of the ragged gap that reached from quarter to stern. A bucket on a rope's end narrowly missed him as he clambered up. The first lieutenant was on the gallery directing the chain of men working to dowse the fire in the after cabins—they had it well in hand, Clow noted. Mr Narbrough saw him and turned.

"*Arabella*?" he demanded sharply.

Clow pushed the dripping hair from his face. To his astonishment, he found himself on the brink of tears.

"She won't—won't move, sir," he choked. "Captain Phillips said he'd do naught without an order in proper form."

Narbrough said nothing. The blackened men passing the buckets heard Clow's words and broke out in a torrent of oaths, consigning the *Arabella* and her captain to hell and naming Phillips "Buckingham's bumboy". The first lieutenant cut them short with two terse words and spoke close to Clow's ear.

"I've to tell you your cousin's dead. He was in the cabin here. And Sir Christopher——" he checked himself and then went on in the same steady voice. "Sir Christopher's below decks. He's dying."

"Fire's out, sir," panted a huge half-naked fellow, padding up to him bucket in hand.

"Give it twelve more buckets where the smoke's rising. Then get back on deck. Come," he added to Clow, and led the way in through the stern-gallery door.

On their right hand light glimmered from the hole in the ship's side, beyond the smoking wreckage of furniture and bulkhead. As they passed through and up to the quarter-deck Narbrough shot brief sentences over his shoulder.

"A musket-ball took him in the throat. He refused to go

c   33

below—held the wound together with his fingers and remained in command. For twenty minutes he was like that. Then he was hit in the upper breast and he fell."

The after-deck was a horrid shambles where dead and wounded lay together in their blood, and the quarter-deck was little better. The master's mate, hurrying towards Narbrough, stumbled over fallen bodies; only two of the poop musketeers remained alive by the rail, and they had lowered their muskets. Clow was suddenly aware that the din of battle was no longer a continuous thunder but a series of irregular explosions.

"They're sheering off, sir!" The master's mate was torn between relief and anxiety. "They've hoisted fores'ls and got canvas on the stump of the main——"

"I can see, Mr Frew," said Narbrough between clenched teeth.

The Dutch flagship was fast drawing away from *Victory*. A strengthening westerly breeze filled the rags of canvas she had managed to hoist and sent the battle-smoke shredding away to leeward so that at last something could be seen of the two fleets. Vessels lay in all directions across the leaden sea, and from the sides of some the smoke of gunfire still belched sporadically; but it was plain that De Ruyter's ships were taking advantage of the breeze and making away eastward, while by ones and twos the English moved slowly in the opposite direction. Across the widening strait to starboard of *Victory*, where broken spars and shapeless fragments of timber littered the fouled water, a few guns fired singly from *Eendracht*'s battle-scarred side.

"She has her bellyful," said the master's mate.

"And we have ours," the first lieutenant said gravely.

Clow's pain and weariness overcame him suddenly. He sank down in a corner under the taffrail and sat there unnoticed, blubbering loudly.

Victory's guns—those that were left of her starboard broadside—roared furiously on for some minutes after *Eendracht* was beyond gunshot, until the half-naked automatons that served them could understand that the fight was over.

The cobblestones of the churchyard were slimy with the sooty rain of London when the twelve men came out of the church, snuffling and wiping their eyes with their sleeves. They were seamen from *Victory*. Clow Shovell was there, and Dick Parr who had constituted himself leader of the party, and other Cockthorpe men. After them emerged two gentlemen finely but soberly dressed; the only persons of quality to attend the funeral service of Sir Christopher Myngs, Knight, of Salthouse in Norfolk. One of these gentlemen was tall and thin, pulling a black cloak round his leanness against the drizzle. The other was small and tubby, with a blotched face in which two notably brilliant eyes did much to redeem the ugliness of a nose like a potato. At sight of them Dick Parr hurried to the verger who had bowed the two away from the church porch and questioned him urgently, thereafter returning to his mates at an unseemly speed.

"Now hold you hard, together," he muttered. "They're Navy gents, same's I said. I'm for tellin' 'em what we was a-sayin' a while ago. All agreed?" A murmur assured him of agreement. "We'll draw down on 'em, then."

The two gentlemen were getting into their waiting coach. As the door closed Dick laid a hand on it and poked his head in.

"Your pardon, sirs. Might a poor seaman have a word?"

The tall man looked at his companion, who nodded eagerly.

"You may speak and welcome, good fellow," he said. "I am Sir William Coventry. This is Mr Pepys, clerk to the Navy Office."

Dick Parr drew breath. He was as good a talker as any man in North Norfolk and he had a little speech ready.

"Sirs," he said, "we are here a dozen of us that ha' long

35

known our dead commander Sir Christopher Myngs—aye, and loved him."

"Aye," muttered the rest, clustered behind him.

"We've laid him in earth, sirs," Dick went on, gaining eloquence as his confidence increased. "We'd give more than the last office, as it's called. We've our lives and naught beside, so we'd give 'em to revenge him. If you'll please to get His Royal Highness to give us a fireship among us all—choose you one to be commander and the rest'll serve him—we'll do that which shall show our memory of Cap'n Chris."

"Aye—aye," said the gruff voices.

Sir William Coventry appeared much moved. Mr Pepys (a gentleman of sentiment) was openly mopping his eyes with a handkerchief but presently stuffed the handkerchief in his pocket while he noted down the names of all present.

"I will do for you what I may," he told them in his high, pleasant voice, "remembering that fireships and commands are mighty scarce, as you know. God be with you!"

The coach clattered away. That night of 13th June 1666 a Diary, now in its sixth year, recorded the incident: "one of the most romantique that ever I heard of," wrote Mr Samuel Pepys in his weird shorthand.

Clow Shovell kept no diary. Only his memory recorded this first meeting with the man who was to influence his life and career more than any other.

TWO

The Karamanli rulers of Barbary sent a letter to King Charles of England. It was a letter of complaint and more than a little peevish in tone. The Deys pointed out (through the Dey of Algiers, who indited the letter) that the English king had neglected to fulfil the terms of the treaty between Algiers, Tunis and Tripoli on the one hand and England on the other, by which the Deys undertook not only to cease attacking English ships and the English ports along the Channel but also to allow all Christian slaves to be ransomed at the current market price. They complained of the delay in sending the ransoms, whereby the owners of Christian slaves, being debarred from selling them on a rising market, were losing legitimate profit.

King Charles was as usual short of money; to do him justice, he was just now spending most of the royal allowance (Mr Pepys joyfully abetting) on new ships for his Navy. But Charles the Second was never at a loss.

"God's buttons!" said he. "The gravamen here is that the slaves are Christians and hopeful of redemption. We will permit the Christian Church to redeem them."

So began a great collection in all the churches of southern England. The people gave freely, especially in Norfolk; many a Norfolk merchant-sailor had been taken and was still held by the Sallee rovers. And in October of that year, 1674, the ransom money was embarked in a squadron of King's ships together with an extra £400 for use as bribes and dispatched to the Mediterranean. The squadron was a small one and weak, for—as Mr Pepys had just informed Parliament—there was not a single ship of the line fit for sea. *Dragon, Assistance, Dartmouth* and *Portsmouth* were fifth-raters of twenty guns or less; *Henrietta* a fourth-rate ship mounting forty guns. The flagship *Harwich*, wearing the flag of Rear-Admiral Sir John Narbrough, carried fifty-six guns and was the most efficient third-rater in the service, due largely to the efforts of her first lieutenant, Clowdisley Shovell. Having passed the Straits without incident, the squadron proceeded off Tunis and there spent the winter and most of the spring while the customary prolonged bargaining with the Dey's agents went on. By March some two hundred Englishmen in varying states of health and spirits (according to the masters they had been assigned by the fortune of the markets) were on their way home in merchant ships. There was no lack of this necessary transport, for English trade in the Mediterranean was increasing rapidly—so fast, indeed, that although the ending of the Dutch wars had released the King's fleets for other duties there were insufficient warships to guard the convoys.

And the convoys required to be guarded. The traders and escort frigates spoken by Narbrough's ships had each a tale of depredation to tell; of loitering merchant ships seized by many-oared galleys darting out like hawks from the desert coast; of desperate actions to beat off the Algerine pirates issuing from Sallee on the Atlantic shore to pursue their centuries-old trade. The stories confirmed the opinions of *Harwich*'s first lieutenant, who had from the first misliked the purpose of this cruise.

"It's as I said, Sir John," he declared stubbornly. "The Turks rule these Moors only by letting them follow their pirate habits. We should be fighting them, not dickering and stickling like Jews."

The admiral was accustomed to tolerate the forthrightness of this somewhat aggressive subordinate. Shovell was his protégé and a Norfolk man; he had watched him grow from boyhood into hard efficient manhood, and the ten years' difference in their ages had not prevented the growth of a close friendship. But there were times when young Clowdisley needed putting in his place.

"I have my commission, as you very well know, Mr Shovell," he said with a frown. "It is to conclude this business as peaceably as I may. I shall ask your advice when I require it."

And Mr Shovell, doffing his feathered hat, had retired in a huff that was acerbated by the knowledge that he had spoken foolishly; he was aware, with sullen resentment of the fact, that his country's Navy was not strong enough to make open war on the North African states. Coming on deck (the squadron lay at anchor off Algiers) he found justifiable vent for his ill temper—a recent stain of tobacco-juice on the scrubbed planking. Men ran with pail and holystone at his furious roar. Lieutenant Shovell had already a reputation for harshness, which to the minds of *Harwich*'s crew was very narrowly balanced by his seamanship and known courage.

This was a different Clowdisley Shovell from the thin-skinned boy of the Four Days' Battle nine years ago. Between the ages of 16 and 25 a man's experience of life moulds him more forcibly than at any other period, and for Clow, at sea with John Narbrough for most of that time, experiences had come crowding. With Sir John he had sailed on the famous voyage of the *Sweepstakes*, a 36-gun ship of 300 tons' burthen, through the Straits of Magellan into the South Seas on a friendly mission to the Spaniards of Chile; he had been in the Battle of Solebay towards the end of the third war with the Dutch, where Narbrough's behaviour—almost the only thing of credit in that disastrous fight—had won his knighthood; Clow had accompanied the King on a tour of inspection round Narbrough's ship at Spithead and had been deeply impressed by Charles's searching questions and comprehensive knowledge of naval details. Nor was this present embassy to the

39

Deys Clow's first visit to the Mediterranean, for as second lieutenant in *Henrietta* he had been with a convoy to Alexandria, fighting off on the way an attack by two pirate galleys out of Tripoli. In brief, Mr Shovell had some ground for conceiving himself a fully fledged seaman, fighting-man, and officer, with golden prospects opening before him.

On the occasion of the King's visit His Majesty's companion had been a squat dark man of an almost comically eager enthusiasm. There had been no recognition of previous acquaintance between Mr Pepys, now Secretary of the Navy, and the tall young lieutenant who strode round the decks with them; but Narbrough had afterwards told him what was said over the wine in the captain's cabin, when Mr Pepys (with whom Sir John was a favourite) had revealed the great plans he was maturing for the Royal Navy, plans backed by all the resources the King could squeeze from a suspicious Parliament. So Clow knew of the thirty new ships now a-building under the direction of Anthony Deane and of the Secretary's determination to create a Navy capable of resisting the powerful fleet of King Louis of France. The new Navy, the Secretary declared, must be bound into unity by the strictest discipline and captained by tried seamen. Clow, approving all this most strongly, perceived in Mr Pepys a man after his own heart, and—a thing more important—a man who could reward a tried seaman and strict disciplinarian like himself. For though he still nursed a shadow of that boyhood vision of a Navy that should make England supreme as a sea-power, it had lately faded before the vision of a supreme sea-officer whose name should be Clowdisley Shovell.

This Clow Shovell, then, had a notably high opinion of himself, and was ready to prove the accuracy of that opinion to all comers. His dress and bearing reflected it. On the morning in late May when the squadron set sail for Tripoli he stood on *Harwich's* quarter-deck arrayed in crimson velvet with ruffles of lace at neck and wrists. Since he disapproved of the bejewelled gallants who were ship's officers by Court favour, his leather thigh-boots were of seamanlike quality and his sword in its worn scabbard had a plain steel hilt. But his wig— for wigs were in—was carefully curled. It framed a round, humourless brown face whose studied lack of expression was relieved by the alertness of the eyes, small and singularly bright beneath level brows. That those eyes missed no piece of un-tidiness or misdemeanour was but too well known to the men under his command, as was the swift retribution that overtook transgressors. If they had no great affection for their first lieutenant they were at least very zealous to obey him, and the spotless decks, the subdued mutter of voices from the waist, and the falls neatly flemished-down at the foot of the main-mast all evidenced the success of Mr Shovell's methods. So did the terse adequacy of the masthead hail at noon.

"Sail fine on the' stabb'd bow, sir . . . headin' toward us, English rig . . . Turkey merchant by her tops'ls."

The squadron was at this time two miles west of Lampedusa island, with a westerly breeze keeping at bay the noonday Mediterranean haze and ruffling the cerulean blue of the sea. They hove-to as the newcomer, a vessel of 600 tons with the Union flag at the main, approached under full sail with the water creaming below her beakhead. As she brought-to half a cable's-length from *Harwich* she lowered a boat, and within five minutes her captain, a large man much agitated, was telling his tale to the admiral.

"We were three ships of the Turkey Company, Sir John— no ship to convoy us—*Hunter* and *Martin* were boarded and taken under my eyes——"

"By whom?" Narbrough demanded.

"Why, by the Tripoli pirates, sir. They were but two miles off Tripoli, coasting toward Misratah. My *Rose* was farther to seaward and so we escaped them. It was but yesterday, Sir John—and *Hunter*'s cargo, calculated at lowest, was worth a good thirty thousand guineas——"

41

Sir John heard him out, grimly assured him that he would take order with the Dey of Tripoli on his arrival there, and advised that *Rose* should proceed to Tunis and await escort through the Straits. Mr Shovell was at his elbow before the *Rose*'s captain was over the ship's side.

"The Dey's broken treaty, sir," he said, with difficulty restraining his excitement. "It's an open declaration of war, an insolent challenge. You'll take it up, sir?"

Narbrough regarded him coldly with eyebrows slightly raised. "One act of piracy does not make a war, Mr Shovell. I shall require the Dey to surrender ships, men, and cargo intact before I open negotiations concerning the ransoms."

"And if he doesn't comply?"

"Then I shall be forced to blockade Tripoli until he does," said the admiral.

II

Tripoli viewed from the sea looked a pleasant enough place. Its massed houses with the big stone fort dominating the centre appeared snowy white in the dazzling sunlight, and the green palms of the coastal oasis made bright contrasting colour with the red-brown of rocky hills behind and the blue sea in front. One wall of the fort, contiguous to the Dey's great palace, rose straight above the harbour basin, with what seemed to be an autumn forest ranged along its base. It was a forest of tall spars and brown sails, for a multitude of ships and galleys lay alongside there beneath the guns of the fort. The harbour, the strongest and safest in the Mediterranean, lay between two peninsulas of brown rock, the western peninsula being the longer and having an artificial stone extension on which stood a smaller fort and a battery. From the eastern side a long stone breakwater curved out to enclose the broad oval of sheltered water. The gap between breakwater and outer fort was partly closed by three moles constructed of rocks, between which there was space only for small boats. Between the easternmost mole and the breakwater, however, there was an entrance just wide enough for the Dey's largest warships. A pleasant place it seemed to the men who saw it from Sir John Narbrough's anchored squadron in May. By August they had begun to hate the sight of it.

For the blockade of Tripoli, which was to last for five months, began as soon as it was plain that the Tripolines intended to hold on to their recent captures at all costs. The old Dey of Tripoli had died a month ago. The new Dey, his son, a fiery stripling of 17, would not be bound by any will but his own. The admiral himself went ashore to the palace on the first embassy, ignoring his lieutenant's protestations that a junior officer could deal with a heathen jackanapes, and learned that he had a difficult problem to solve. Narbrough had powers from the King's own hand to amend or alter the existing treaty and he was ready to make concessions; he knew very well that the last thing the King or the Parliament wanted was war with Barbary, and an ultimatum backed by threat of invasion meant war with Algiers and Tunis as well as with Tripoli. The man who caused that was ruined for life —indeed, might be deprived of life as well as of reputation. He made successive offers, refraining from any denouncement of the latest piracy but including the restitution of *Hunter* and *Martin* in his terms. The young Dey listened, sneered, returned patently insulting answers which the interpreter translated in more courtly terms. In the end he turned his back. And the admiral retired with what dignity he could muster.

After waiting a week for the Dey or his advisers to see reason, Sir John went again to the palace. The interview took the same course as before, but this time it had a different ending.

"Your Highness needs time for the consideration of my terms," Narbrough said, his stern eye bidding the interpreter translate as precisely as he might. "I can wait, and so can my ships. I regret that it will not be possible for any vessels to enter or leave Your Highness's harbour while we are waiting."

43

With that he turned on his heel and was out of the audience room before the Dey could reply.

Sir John Narbrough had an endless patience (Mr Shovell found it exasperating) and a bulldog disregard for discomfort once he took hold. While the burning summer weeks crawled past he lay with his ships across the seaward gate of Tripoli, little troubled to find himself faced by a stubbornness equal to his own. The Tripolines could not be starved into submission —there were coastal and oasis towns to supply them with the bare necessities—but he knew that their losses in seaborne trade must be crippling. All the merchants of the port, not to mention the owners of pirate galleys, must be clamouring against the growing threat of poverty; sooner or later the Dey must yield to their demands. Perhaps he underestimated the power of an autocrat in a land where men could be tortured or beheaded for the Dey's amusement. At any rate, the year ran on into autumn without any sign from the blockaded town.

The days were not without incident, nor were the ships idle. On four occasions Tripoli galleys came over the horizon, making for their home port, and the two fastest of the fifth-rate ships were detached to chase them; in vain, for with their banks of oars to aid the huge lateen sails the galleys had the heels of them. Narbrough kept *Harwich* and two ships besides on blockade service and used the others in turn as messengers, supply ships, and convoy escorts for passing merchantmen, thus giving the flagship little opportunity for action but affording his first lieutenant much opportunity for drilling the men. *Harwich* hoisted and took in sail, beat to quarters, sent away boats and hauled them inboard again with such frequency and repetition that the Dey, if he was watching from the arched windows of his palace, must have thought Allah had caused the infidels to be possessed of devils. Clowdisley Shovell could, and did, perform every action required in these manœuvres better than any of his men; which Mr Frew, the staid second lieutenant, thought unbefitting. Dick Parr the bo'sun, on the other hand, thanked his stars for a first lieutenant who was also a seaman. From being Clow's senior messmate Dick had become his most devoted admirer.

Clow's intense activity was his way of relieving the pressure of his impatience. In after years he was to inspire a fo'c's'le rhymester to a much-quoted couplet:

> *When Shovell's made to wait*
> *A fight will be our fate,*

and it may be that the long Tripoli blockade taught him this kind of patience. Violent action was the only argument the Dey could understand. But no amount of pestering from his juniors would shift Sir John; and Clow, knowing this, kept silence.

In August dispatches from the Navy Board arrived, brought by three small ships. There was a letter from Mr Samuel Pepys acknowledging Narbrough's report, dispatched by a westbound convoy a month earlier, and regretting that he had only three small vessels to send for his command. He hoped Sir John might find use for them as fireships if a peaceable solution of the Tripoli problem—which he prayed God would yet provide—could not be arrived at. Since it was inconceivable that any hostile ship could pass the entrance and cross the harbour without being sunk, the reinforcement added nothing to Narbrough's powers of persuasion. One of the vessels, *Sapphire*, had on board a young spark named Matthew Aylmer, the 17-year-old son of Sir Christopher Aylmer of Balrath in Ireland, lately page to the Duke of Buckingham and sent to sea to expiate some knavery or other. If the knavery was sufficiently outrageous to anger George Villiers, thought Mr Shovell when he heard this, it must have been black indeed.

The augmented squadron continued to lie well outside the range of the big cannon in the fort. No shots were fired by either side. The only signs of hostile confrontation were the guard-boats patrolling from sunset to sunrise, one round the

45

cluster of anchored ships and the other to and fro just inside the harbour entrance. From a distance Tripoli seemed to sleep through the shortening October days. But on the last day of that month came evidence that the Dey or his servants were very wide awake.

It was Sir John's custom every week or so to up anchor and hoist sail and make what the hands called "Narby's half-mile cruise"—taking the squadron along to westward and back again to their blockade stations without going out of sight of the harbour entrance. On this occasion he took advantage of a southerly breeze, warm for the time of year, which fell suddenly to a dead calm as the squadron reached its farthest point and made to go about. With unusual rapidity (it was rumoured in *Harwich* that the Dey's marabouts had produced it) a dense fog formed, and in cover of it four large galleys slipped out of Tripoli harbour, passing so close to the becalmed English ships that the beat of their oars could be heard.

The escape was a misfortune on more than one count. Sir John had news that a convoy of merchantmen sailing from the Levant would be off Tripoli within the next seven days; he was to provide escort through the Straits. Four Tripoli galleys at large in search of prey might encounter that convoy, in which case there would be nothing left for his ships to escort— there was even a possibility that the Tripolines knew of it already and this daring break was the result. *Dragon*, *Assistance* and *Dartmouth* were ordered to sail and meet the convoy, and with the first sign of a breeze they were away. Less disturbing but equally annoying was the probable effect of the galleys' success upon the ruler of Tripoli. An unbreakable blockade might have inclined the Dey to capitulate; knowledge that it could be broken would certainly influence him to prolong his resistance. Sir John deliberated long and alone. Then, with a touch of resignation in his manner, he invited Lieutenant Clowdisley Shovell to deliberate with him. Two hours and three bottles of Maltese wine later a plan had been made.

On a November morning of bright sun and cool breeze *Harwich*'s longboat approached the harbour entrance. In her stern sheets was Mr Shovell clad in crimson velvet, standing erect so that the lopping of the little waves should not wet his breeches; he was the better able to stand that the longboat was proceeding very slowly. The Tripoli guard-boat challenged, was answered by a wave of Mr Shovell's feathered hat and a shout of "The Dey!", and drew aside to let the boat creep on across the harbour to the quays. Clow's sharp eyes had made careful note of the guard-boat: its long narrow build somewhat resembling a Malta *dghaisa*, its crew of four armed with muskets and long curved knives. They made careful note of all that was to be seen as the longboat pulled at leisurely speed towards the crowded shipping beneath the walls of fort and palace. On the walls, where armed men thronged chattering to watch him land, thin spirals of smoke betokened burning match, implying that the row of great cannon up there were maintained in continuous readiness. Lying alongside directly beneath the cannon were four fine ships, not war galleys like those that had escaped, but three-masters pierced for cannon and of such size that they could barely squeeze through the harbour entrance. The largest was a 50-gun ship, the others hardly smaller. He could identify two rather smaller vessels moored in the eastern bay as the captured merchant ships *Hunter* and *Martin*.

A greybeard in white robes received him with grave ceremony as he stepped from boat to quay. Clow touched his hat and continued to dart quick glances round him. A long row of smaller craft lay at the quay on either side of the four ships, cockboats and fishing-craft and small coasters packed beam-to-beam. On the quay itself a longer row of sheds or shelters, open-sided, housed cargo waiting for shipment—stores, food-stuffs, bales.

"*Effendi!* The Dey waits your presence," said the greybeard in fair English. "If you will please to follow me——"

"Lead on," said Clow.

He was glad they had no farther to go than a hundred paces, across the quay to a flight of wide steps and a big arched doorway in the palace wall. Tripoli under one's nose was a deal less pleasant than it had appeared from a distance. It stank. The deserted appearance of the quay, which had surprised him as he came ashore, was explained by the two close rows of armed men on either hand, holding back the thronging crowd of Tripolines at the distance of a long stone's throw. These soldiers of the Dey, barefooted and wearing the caftan, nevertheless handled their muskets as if they knew how to use them, and so did the two guards inside the arched doorway.

The greybeard led him through a gloomy stone antechamber, deserted, into a smaller room hung with silks and dimly lit by perfumed lamps. Here, with an obeisance, he motioned Clow to wait and vanished through the long curtains at one end of the room, reappearing almost at once to beckon the lieutenant past him into a larger chamber beyond. This room was stuffy with heat and the scent of musk. A gaudy tiled floor was strewn with rugs and cushions, and on more cushions at the farther end reclined the Dey of Tripoli, an overfat youth in a loose saffron robe. The Dey appeared in no haste to finish his sport with two shapely girls who shared his cushions. Lieutenant Shovell swept off his feathered hat and stood rigidly erect with one hand resting on his sword-hilt, his resentment at this cavalier treatment somewhat softened by the sight of female charms so lavishly displayed. At the end of a minute the Dey banished his giggling companions with a wave of his hand and snapped a sentence or two at the greybeard; whose role, it appeared, was to be that of interpreter, for he made a salaam to his master and then turned to translate to the English envoy.

"His Highness asks if you are come to say farewell. He asks why you did not catch his four galleys when they left the harbour."

Mr Shovell was there to deliver an ultimatum and had no intention of bandying words. He spoke in a voice that would have carried from bow to stern of *Harwich* in a gale, allowing bare time between sentences for the interpreter to translate.

"The King of England has been very patient. His patience is at an end. Your Highness has three days more to accept the terms offered by the King's admiral. If the admiral has had no word from you at the end of three days he will begin to strike blows at Tripoli. Each blow will be harder than the one before it. They will continue until your Highness agrees to the English terms, and"—he lapsed into broad Norfolk—"that'll jibbuck yer cockles up, bor!"

On that he clapped his hat on his head, swung round, and marched out of the room without waiting to hear whether the interpreter made anything of his final remark.

His jaunty bearing as he passed through the outer chambers concealed a certain apprehension. In his own estimation Lieutenant Clowdisley Shovell would make a very important hostage; and while the Dey probably knew he would get no backing from Tunis or Algiers if he broke irrevocably with England he might, just possibly, take the risk of seizing and holding this unceremonious ambassador. But no one stopped him. The guards saluted untidily as he passed out of the archway into the blinding sunlight of the quays, and he crossed the clear space between the palace steps and his boat without a soul coming near him. The Dey's guards were still keeping back the murmuring crowds, the longboat and her crew had not been molested. In half an hour he was reporting to Sir John Narbrough that the first stage in their joint plan was completed.

The three days of grace expired without sign or message. On the morning of the fourth day the four pinnaces of the squadron, oars manned by picked men, mustered in line abreast under the lee of the flagship, each with its jack flying in the stern sheets. A cannon boomed on board *Harwich* and the four boats

D

began to pull furiously for the land—not for the harbour but for the strip of beach below the rocky ridge half a mile west of the walled town. The race had been announced by the admiral two days earlier and Sir John had promised a prize of twenty pieces-of-eight to the boat that should first land a man on the beach. To this had been added an unofficial competition, devised among themselves by the officers in charge of the boats: the winner would be he who planted the English colours farthest inland on the Dey's territory. There was no prize for this save honour.

While the rival pinnaces ploughed their converging furrows across the flat blue surface, beetle-like shapes diminishing towards the red-gold line of the shore to the right of Tripoli's ancient walls, the admiral kept his quarter-deck. His perspective glass was at his eye; he watched, not the racing boats, but the walls and quays and dingy outskirts of Tripoli. It was inconceivable that on this first day after his ultimatum's expiry the Dey and his men should not be on the alert. He could make out a bustling movement on the walls, but that was all at first—until his glass wavered rightward and he saw a thin irregular mass moving out below the walls along the low ridge, like a white wave lapping across the red rocks, dividing into thinner rivulets as the white-robed warriors took up position along the crest. Sir John lowered the glass and rubbed his chin, frowning. He hoped Shovell would not forget his purpose.

Shovell had at any rate forgotten his dignity. In the stern-sheets of *Harwich*'s pinnace, with a lead of three lengths over his nearest rival, he was bellowing at his straining crew in the wildest excitement. Wig and velvet coat were left behind for this diversion and he was young Clow Shovell of Cockthorpe again. A swift glance astern roused a yet louder bellow and a rare burst of language.

"They're gaining! Pull, ye dunghill bastards! Lay to it, ye sons of whores!"

The brawny oarsmen accepted this adjuration in the spirit in which it was intended. They tugged at the heavy oars till the looms bent, and rammed her forefoot into the soft sand a few seconds before *Sapphire*'s pinnace did the same. The force of the impact sent them sprawling backwards off the thwarts and pitched Shovell from his place in the stern, but the big lieutenant converted his fall into a headlong leap overside into the shallows. Pausing only to wrest the Union flag from its socket, he splashed at a gallop towards the thin rim of dry sand. Close behind him came the officer from *Sapphire*'s boat, also with a flag.

Above the beach a jumble of red-brown boulders ran up to the bare glacis of rock below the crest. On that jagged skyline a row of heads bobbed and peered. Clow saw them, glanced behind him, and ran on. He struck the butt of the jackstaff between two rocks half-way up the glacis just as a musket banged from the crest. The leaden ball hummed past his left ear. A slim figure in coat and breeches of bright blue camlet ran past his other side, up the slope—young Aylmer of the *Sapphire*, clutching a great feathered hat to his head with one hand and brandishing a Union flag in the other. In the same instant a score of muskets exploded and the air seemed full of flying bullets. Aylmer stumbled on.

Clow loosed his flag, sprang after him, swung him roughly round with a hand on his shoulder.

"Back, you young fool!" he roared. "Back to the boats!"

Aylmer turned a handsome, impish face. His grin showed white teeth and his black eyes glinted wickedly.

"You've dropped your flag, Mr Shovell," he said. "I call upon you to witness—this."

He drove the jackstaff into a crack in the rocks. As he did so his feathered hat sailed from his head and another bullet whined in ricochet from the stones at their feet. Clow wrenched the flag out and thrust it into Aylmer's hand. His grip fastened on the lad's arm and he rushed him down towards the beach,

51

catching up his own banner as they ran. Muskets were firing all along the crest now. The soft sand beyond the boulders spurted in little fountains about their flying feet. Two of the pinnaces were already pulling back to the ships, and the crews from *Harwich* and *Sapphire* were ready to lay to their oars the moment their errant officers came splashing up to tumble in over the stern. From behind them came a piercing chorus of yells from the white-robed men leaping down from the crest.

When the boats were out of range of the ineffective musketry from the beach Matthew Aylmer called across the intervening water to *Harwich*'s boat.

"Mr Shovell! If it please you, am I to be invited to dinner tonight?"

"Tonight?" Clow was never quick at the taking-up of another's wit.

"At midnight, as I understand—a hot meal. I'd thought to qualify as a fire-eater."

Mr Shovell saw the point now. He chuckled.

"Your company, sir, will be desired, I do assure you," he returned. "We dine indeed—at midnight."

III

At midnight the sea was a still black mirror beneath a tapestry of black velvet hung with sequins. There was no moon. Everywhere the smooth surface glimmered with the reflections of the stars, except where small moving shapes crept shoreward, leaving rows of dancing silver specks in their wakes. "*I shall employ all the boats of the squadron, twelve in number, each under a considerable officer: my lieutenant Clowdisley Shovell to be commander-in-chief of them all.*" So ran the message to all captains from the admiral. Narbrough had *Harwich, Henrietta* and *Dartmouth*, with the three fireships, left of his original fleet, and these had supplied nine of the boats; two merchantmen waiting for convoy to Scanderoon had provided the others. Lieutenant Shovell had himself taken copies of the message to every ship

52

and had spent much time with the picked crews and the gunners, for he required a precise performance of his plan and an exact obedience to his orders. The boats that crawled across the starry water towards Tripoli moved silently, every oar muffled in its rowlock with wrappings of cloth. Six of them steered a half-circle course starting to eastward, six started to westward, but both flotillas turned at length so as to gain the shelter of the harbour breakwater on either side of the entrance. There was a bare possibility that some sharp-eyed soldier on the fortress walls might discern the dark specks far out by the anchored ships, but a watcher at sea-level within the harbour would have no chance of seeing their circuitous approach.

The four Tripoli warriors in the guard-boat kept what they considered an adequate watch. With one man at the oars, the boat pulled gently back and forth a short pistol-shot inside the harbour entrance, occasionally pausing while the oarsman rested and his companions peered into the darkness beyond the stone bastions of the entrance. They expected nothing and saw nothing. The blockading Franks had made their foolish attack that morning, on the west beach, and had run away. It was unlikely that they would attack again so soon—and if they did, they had no hope of success. An enemy boat must come in by the entrance and the guards would see it in time to fire muskets and pull for the quays. Then the matches that showed tiny red eyes on the walls of the fort would go to the touch-holes of the Dey's cannon and the silly Franks would be smashed to pieces. The men in the guard-boat hoped that would not happen, for they were more afraid of their comrades' shooting than of the Franks.

The oarsman rested on his oars for the twentieth time. The others looked casually out at the starlit sea beyond the entrance. There was a swirl of movement in the water under the gunwale as twelve muscular hands reached up to fasten on it all along the boat's side. One startled exclamation, instantly stilled as water filled the open mouth, and the guard-boat capsized as suddenly as if she had been overthrown by a tornado. The rest of the business was done under water, so that apart from the first wallowing splash—hardly more than the noise made by an oarsman missing his stroke—there was no sound loud enough to disturb the sentinels in the fort. By ones and twos six heads broke surface. The swimmers trod water while four of them sheathed the knives at their waist-belts.

"Muckwash, that is," muttered Dick Parr, spitting harbour water.

"Silence!" hissed Lieutenant Shovell angrily.

He was looking towards the black line of the breakwater whence he and his five picked men had swum under water to the guard-boat. A dim white square showed itself and vanished; the man he has posted there with a white flag was signalling that the boats were about to come in. He swam a few strokes away from the entrance and the others moved until they were spaced in line on his left, at five-yard intervals. As the first six boats glided into the harbour the swimmers boarded over their sterns in order, not without a certain amount of noise as their naked bodies were hauled into the sternsheets. Clow Shovell, pushing his wet legs into his breeches, strained his ears anxiously for the sound of an alarm; there was none. Cherry, the master's mate, handed him his sword in silence and he buckled it on, careful to avoid knocking blade or hilt against the thwart. All the eleven boats astern of him were in line and a boat's-length apart; he could just make that out in the starlight, and see the ninth boat lead off to larboard when they were half-way across the harbour, as he had ordered. Halfway across—and still no alarm. It must come at any moment now. The wall of the fort bulked huge against the stars, with a tiny red glow here and there on the battlements. A cry, followed instantly by a shot, came from over on his left where the four boats were making for the store-sheds on the quay.

"Pull, now!" he snapped at the rowers. "Hull yourselves bodily into it!"

The leading boat and its seven followers leapt forward to the beat of straining oars. Overhead the spars of the four big ships alongside grew against the starry heaven. Two boats to each ship they boarded, swarming up the tumblehome sides to hand the parcels of combustibles from one to another. Muskets clattered and banged from farther along the quay and a swelling chorus of yells sounded dispersedly from the quayside buildings. Clow, sword in hand on the after-deck of the 50-gun ship, peered alertly round him for any sign of resistance on board and, seeing none, felt exultation rise in him. He had brought 157 men within pistol-shot of the Dey's palace to do this work and it was now certain that it would be done. He turned, with his back to the cabin door under the poop, to watch the fire-party busy on the fore-deck; and as he did so a slight figure darted past him from his front. There was a clang and a clash, a heavy thud. He swung round, to see the slight figure standing above a white-robed heap. Starshine glinted on the steel of a fallen scimitar.

"The point's the thing against these butcher-cleavers," said Matt Aylmer coolly; he drew his sword-blade between his fingers and flipped the blood aside. "You were about to be cleft apart, Mr Shovell—half-a-Clow to larboard, half-a-Clow to starboard."

The jest was not to Mr Shovell's liking but this was no time to say so. "You've my thanks, sir," he said. "I owe you——"

A thunderous explosion, above and close at hand, cut him short. Another followed, and another. The fort cannon had opened fire, presumably shooting blindly into the harbour waters. A wavering orange glow was lighting the stone wall of the fortress above them—the store-sheds were ablaze, and a line of fire spread along the small craft at the quayside below them. Clow sprang up the ladder to the poop for a quick survey. Flames were licking up from the 'tween-decks of the two ships next in line to his, and the vessel beyond them was vomiting reddened smoke from her ports.

55

"We ha' done, sir!" yelled Dick Parr's voice from the foot of the ladder. "A right job, that is!"

A volcano of fire spurting from the 50-gun ship's forehatch confirmed his words. Clow pulled his whistle from his breeches pocket and blew one long shrill blast. Then he was down at the bulwarks urging his men overside into the waiting boats. Before he swung down himself, the last to leave, the heat of the flames was scorching his naked back.

Twelve boats raced for the harbour entrance across waters that were no longer black but red. By the noise it seemed that every musket in Tripoli was firing at them. The uproar of shots and shouts was punctuated at intervals by the boom of cannon; but the firing was wild, and none of the iron balls came near them. Twelve boats mustered outside the harbour, and from their sternsheets as they pulled back in line to the squadron their officers watched the flames leap higher and higher at the quaysides. The first blow struck by the King's admiral had been a hard one indeed. There should be no need for a second.

And in due course the Dey capitulated. He sued for terms, and they were given as he deserved, from the victors to the vanquished. In addition to *"Release of all the English captives resyding in the cytty and kingdom of Tripoli, without ransom"*, he was required to hand over the sum of 80,000 dollars to the admiral. This being done, Sir John employed the whole sum in ransoming Christian slaves of other nations, including many Maltese. He also distributed 1,956 pieces-of-eight among the 157 men who had taken part in the expedition, Lieutenant Clowdisley Shovel receiving the lion's share, 80 pieces—which was no more than his deserts and indeed considerably less in Mr Shovell's private opinion.

"Such was the wonderful mercy of Almighty God towards us," wrote the admiral in conclusion of his dispatch to the Navy Board, *"that not one man of ours was killed, wounded or touched, nor a boat any ways disabled, but all returned in safety."* The first

lieutenant, to whom he showed the dispatch before sending it, approved the praise of Lieutenant Clowdisley Shovell in its earlier pages, but secretly considered this concluding statement unnecessary and even inaccurate. Had it not been (he told himself resentfully) for the genius of Clowdisley Shovell, his exact planning, his stern insistence on absolute discipline, his inspired leadership—had all these not been present at Tripoli the mercy of Almighty God would have done precious little for the expedition. He went off in *Harwich*'s cockboat to dine with Matthew Aylmer, and two bottles of Cyprus wine combined with Aylmer's flattery to confirm this opinion to his entire satisfaction.

THREE

Mr Samuel Pepys records in his shorthand journal for the year 1684—the last he ever kept—certain shameful doings of Vice-Admiral Arthur Herbert; how Herbert promoted his *valet de chambre* and partner in vice to command a King's ship; how he and his officers debauched for a whole month together off the Portuguese coast, with loose women on board; how, before this company, Herbert stripped the fleet surgeon stark naked and hung him by the leg from the deckhead in his cabin to be mocked; and how he was accustomed to address his chaplain publicly as "Ballocks". This was the man to whom Sir John Narbrough handed over the Mediterranean squadron when he sailed for England; and a more complete change in command could hardly have been achieved.

Herbert represented the barrier that confronted the little Secretary in his struggle to create a strong Navy. Unstable and inconstant, capable of reckless bravery and heartless cruelty, he held rank by virtue of the powerful family of which he was a member. He was so little of a seaman that he could not name the sheets and halyards in his flagship *Dragon*, and a typical order from the quarter-deck was a volley of foul oaths followed by "Haul on that whichum there!" With the Barbary states held to an uneasy peace, his chief task in the Mediterranean was to chastise the Moorish pirates that harassed the merchantmen plying to Tangier, where King Charles had established a base. Anchored off Tangier with his squadron, Admiral Herbert summoned all captains to a conference on board *Dragon*; to which, with the others, came Captain Matthew Aylmer and Captain Clowdisley Shovell.

The big stern cabin was hung with stained Padua silks and stank of spilt wine. Below the carved and gilded royal arms on the bulkhead was nailed a lewd picture filched from a Malaga *bagnio*. The admiral's one good eye—the other had been lost in a duel with an Algerine corsair—leered at his officers from a visage sallow and unprepossessing under its elaborate wig.

"Some of you", he said without preamble, "will be bloody Papists and some bloody Protestants. I care not a turd. I'd have you know the Pope or the Parliament may be uppermost for me, so long as I'm comfortable."

The captains grinned askance at each other but with understanding. This was apposite matter, for at home in England it was "the jealous time", the era of Popish plots and counterplots with Catholic and Protestant snarling and snapping at each other like two dogs on the leash.

"Serve me and I'll serve you," continued the admiral; he leaned forward across the oaken table, scanning the circle of sun-tanned faces with his single eye. "Harkee, gentlemen. You'll fight these poxy Moors when you meet 'em, which will be precious seldom. You'll win glory, devil doubt you for that, but you'll win no money. So. You'll have heard of Good Voyages, maybe?"

Pearce of the *Sapphire* spoke up. "Aye, sir. Sir Edward Spragge, he sent on Good Voyages. Forty per cent was what he gave."

"I'll give fifty," Herbert said instantly. "Attend me, now. While I'm on this station two ships at a time can be at Cadiz, turn and turn about. Watering and re-rigging, you'll understand." He winked grotesquely. "The Dons pay high for cargoes transported by English warships and highest for carrying treasure from port to port. Ship your cargoes, take your pay, report back here and hand over half your profits. The rest's yours. Well?"

He leaned back in his chair, eyeing the assembled captains.

Most showed anticipatory pleasure at this prospect of fortune, but on one or two faces there was a trace of doubt and perhaps of disgust. Herbert thumped the table irritably.

"God damn me! Hasn't a ship's captain a right to a Good Voyage now and again? Can you make a fortune out of a poxy ten shillings a day? Isn't a Good Voyage all in the way of duty?" He settled his wig, which had fallen askew, and spoke more soberly. "There'll be convoy duty for all of you, plenty of it. Use your judgement when you're sent to a port to bring away a convoy. Fill your holds at the biggest price you can get—and, by God, don't sail until you've got it!"

His one-eyed glare went round the circle and found acquiescence, growing enthusiasm. Admiral Herbert roared for his steward to bring glasses and wine. And then more wine. The captains of the Mediterranean fleet returned to their ships more than a little fuddled but well content with their new commander-in-chief. Captain Aylmer was more than content.

"Here's a lad will fill our pockets, Clow," he confided exultantly. "He knows what's due to gentlemen—and to wenches too, by God! Did you hear his tale of the three mulatto girls? God's breath, he could show even George Villiers a rakehelly trick or two!"

Captain Shovell's hearty assent was not entirely sincere; but he was in some things a disciple of Matt Aylmer's nowadays and tended more and more to follow his lead. Since Aylmer regarded naval service as a means to pleasure and excitement, and could see no farther than that, his friend was led slowly but surely away from his old vision of a great Navy in which great seamen might be proud to serve.

The two had become boon companions since the Tripoli affair. Narbrough had given both of them their captaincies in the following year, and in return for Shovell's imparting of the seaman's craft the one-time page of the Duke of Buckingham had instructed him in such matters as the ways of brothels and the art of getting gentlemanly drunk; matters, as he remarked with some truth, of the first importance to any man who hoped one day to present himself at Court. When Sir John returned to England with his squadron (it was the hard winter of 1677, when the King drove his sleigh round St James's Park in deep snow) Clow put his newly acquired knowledge into practice under Matt's guidance. That he found the surfeit of wine and wenches little to his taste was in part due to his dislike of all that was not orderly but more to his discovery that London knew him as a hero. Someone showed him a copy of Mr Muddiman's *Intelligence* wherein the news-writer remarked that all England was thrilling to the news of Lieutenant Shovell's exploit at Tripoli. Captain Shovell began to feel that such a notability should not find himself, or be found by anyone else, reeling away from Mrs Wardle's bawdy-house at three in the morning. An attempt to mend his ways was greatly strengthened after a formal dinner-party at Sir John Narbrough's house. Sir John had invited him in order to inform him that the squadron, with Mr Shovell as captain of the *James*, 30 guns, would sail for the Mediterranean in a week's time, and that his request to have Dick Parr as boatswain was granted; but for Clow the be-all and end-all of the party was the presence of Elizabeth Hill, who looked on him with kind brown eyes and was clearly far too good for a low fellow who had consorted with whores. He did not see her again before the squadron sailed, and the unwonted humility he had felt in her presence melted quickly under the hot Mediterranean sun. So did his other resolutions. Matt Aylmer (now commanding the 30-gun *Charles*) regained his ascendancy.

There was some fighting to be done, as well as the escorting of convoys through the pirate-infested Straits. To Captain Shovell's lot fell the capture, after a savage struggle, of a 32-gun Algerine pirate cruiser whose name—the *Half-Moon*—made an odd addition to the Navy List of 1682 when she became a King's ship. Captain Aylmer distinguished himself in the destruction of five Moorish galleys caught landing troops for an attack on Tangier. Both captains had to their credit a score of lesser fights, and chases almost innumerable, by the time Sir John Narbrough handed over his command to Admiral Herbert and sailed for England to become a Commissioner of the Navy.

It was many months before *James* and *Charles* took their turn, under Admiral Herbert's astute commercial plan, at a Good Voyage to Cadiz, though they had taken convoys to and from the Spanish port often enough in Narbrough's time. Shovell and Aylmer knew Cadiz well (its back streets rather better than the Alameda) and amused themselves by cultivating a lofty contempt for all Spaniards; a nation, said Aylmer, whose filthy beggars gave themselves the airs of Dons while the Dons were as filthy as the beggars. Mr Shovell, however, had made —at a price—one little friend in Cadiz. Juanita of the long smooth limbs and sloe-black eyes was lady's maid in a large house in the Calle Real. Mr Shovell looked forward to combining profitable business with at least one night's pleasure.

A brisk Levanter helped the two small ships to cover the thirty leagues to Cadiz in less than a day's sailing, and they anchored under the guns of Puntales Castle with English colours flying at the masthead. This in the port of a friendly country was a direct contravention of international law. It was Matt Aylmer's suggestion, made over the second bottle— when, as usual, he was at his most outrageous. When his friend demurred:

"God's breath, man!" said he. "Isn't it plain dishonesty to hide our opinions? We know we're better than they are and they shall see that we know it."

So the colours flew in Cadiz harbour, in the face of some dozen ships of the Spanish fleet who were moored there alongside. The Spanish officer who came off in the flagship's boat to remind them, with extreme politeness, of the courtesy to be observed between nations was rudely sent packing by Aylmer. He and Captain Shovell then had themselves rowed ashore—

to be confronted at the top of the harbour steps by a glittering posse of officers headed by the Spanish admiral himself. The admiral, too, was extremely polite. He deprecated, he apologized, he was wounded to the heart at having to say this, but if the English ships did not conform to the rule insisted upon by England herself the guns of the castle would be forced to fire upon them. Captain Aylmer looked at Captain Shovell, whose round face was red as a furnace. Together they swept off their great feathered hats, together turned and went back to their boat. Five minutes later the English mastheads were bare of flags.

James and *Charles* remained at Cadiz for a fortnight without finding any cargo worth embarking. Since they were small ships, it had to be something compact as well as valuable, such as plate or bullion; and until the Flota, the treasure fleet from the Indies, arrived there would be nothing of this sort to be carried. A third week passed and the ships still lay idle. Their captains swaggered about Cadiz in gaudy finery of ruffles and silks and gold braid, ogling the women and shouldering the men out of their way in the manner of the all-conquering sea-captains they conceived themselves to be. This bravado, somewhat beyond their usual behaviour, was a natural but childish reaction to the shame of being forced to haul down their colours. There was perhaps some excuse for Aylmer, who was only 25, but Shovell at 34 should have known better.

It may be that Shovell did know better. At least he knew himself a fool for agreeing to Aylmer's silly trick with the flags, thus contemning the very order and ceremony he approved as the framework of naval discipline. His swaggering concealed a growing disgust with himself; and this was not lessened when he observed, in a coach that passed the *posada* where he was drinking alone one evening, three gentlemen of whom one was incontestably the Secretary of the Navy.

Captain Shovell was not greatly surprised to see Mr Samuel

Pepys in Cadiz, though his presence on this side of the Straits could hardly have been expected. Admiral Herbert's squadron had three months ago exchanged salutes with a small fleet of ships arriving at Tangier. Admiral Lord Dartmouth and the Secretary were on board Sir John Berry's flagship *Grafton*; it was known that these high personages had been sent by the King to wind up the affairs of Tangier and destroy its fortifications preparatory to its abandonment as an English base, and it was not so very odd that Mr Pepys should seize the opportunity of a brief visit to Spain. But the sight of the tubby little man who was toiling to make the Navy of Clow's dreams, who had once—unprepossessing though he was—seemed to Lieutenant Shovell a leader worth following, was an added irritant to a conscience already uneasy.

This small incident doubtless strengthened the effect of the excoriation he was to undergo later that day. At the moment, however, Captain Shovell sought to dismiss it from his thoughts, aiding himself in this with another quartel of wine and the anticipation of this evening's assignation with Juanita at the house in the Calle Real.

II

At half an hour before midnight Captain Shovell was standing shivering in an alcove of Juanita's bedroom, holding the concealing curtain across it with one hand and fastening his breeches with the other. From a few paces away on the other side of the curtain a woman's voice was speaking in good clear English.

"—a monstrous bad headache, Juanita. Mr Hodges and the gentlemen talking, talking, talking, until I vow and protest I could bear it no—God-a-mercy, girl, what a chaos your room is in! But no matter. Put on your gown and attend me to bed. Bring the candle."

A muffled assent seemed to indicate that Juanita was hastily pulling her gown over her head. The faint light beyond the

64

curtain shrank and vanished, leaving Captain Shovell in stuffy darkness. The door closed. Muttering curses, he stooped to grope for the hat and sword the girl had thrust in after him a second before her mistress entered; then he stepped through the curtain into the dark little room and stood listening.

Juanita had told him at their first meeting that her mistress was wife to an English merchant-banker named Hodges, which explained her smattering of the English tongue. He had attached little importance to the information then; but now, with detection so narrowly escaped, he realized the perils of his situation. Discovery in a Spanish household he could have brazened out comfortably, but to be found wenching in the house of an Englishman of standing—he, captain of a King's ship!—was a thing to wound both pride and reputation beyond repair. It was the devil's own luck that Mrs Hodges's headache has hastened her bedtime. Juanita, for reasons best known to herself, had appointed an early assignation; there was to be a dinner-party, she would not be needed for three hours after she had dressed and powdered her mistress, and Mrs Hodges had fixed midnight as the hour when she would leave the gentlemen to their wine and go to bed. Three knocks on the little side-door in the alley, then, at half an hour after nine . . . Thank God the woman's headache didn't overcome her thirty minutes sooner, thought Captain Shovell.

He moved cautiously to the door and opened it. Elaborate iron scrollwork on the railing of a narrow landing showed in silhouette against lamplight somewhere below. Voices and the clatter of dishes came up to his ears, swelling and fading again as doors were opened and closed. The girl had led him up the wide marble stairs he could see below the landing, having first brought him through a maze of dark passages from the side-door. He moved silently down from the landing to the staircase and descended it on tiptoe with a wary eye on the stone-flagged hallway at its foot. The lantern on its wrought-iron bracket cast a dim glow on frescoed walls where no less than five arched doorways offered exit—one of them had a strip of light showing beneath it indicating, probably, a passage leading to the kitchens. Four choices, then; and he could not for the life of him remember which of the four led to the side-door in the alley. Recollecting that the alley ran below the south wall of the house, Captain Shovell called on his seaman's sense of compass directions and decided that the doorway directly opposite the foot of the stairs led southward. He was half-way across the hall to it when yellow light flooded from the opened kitchen door and footsteps and loud voices sent him dashing for cover.

No door closed the dark passage into which he had bolted. He sensed rather than saw a cavernous opening in the wall of the passage on his right, with descending steps revealed by the growing radiance behind him. A man's voice spoke harshly in execrable Spanish, ordering someone to stay by the cellar and bring the bottles from the end bin as they were called for. "The end bin, you yellow-bellied hound—savvy?" added the voice in English.

Captain Shovell had come to a flimsy swing-door ten paces along the passage. He slipped through it at the instant when the two servants reached the passage-end, struck his foot against some object that gave forth a dull ringing sound, and halted rigid with apprehension behind the door. He heard footsteps retreating, then some muttered Spanish objurgations from the man who had been left on duty by the cellar. His sigh of relief was premature. A moment later he perceived, by the light filtering through an oblong of hanging draperies on his left, that he was in even worse case than he had been in Juanita's wardrobe.

He was in the retiring-closet. As in some English mansions, it was at one end of the big dining-room, a mere cupboard behind curtains. The object he had nearly stumbled over was a chamber-pot, and there were two others on a shelf at the back of the closet, which was about four feet square and had no exit except by the way he had come or through the curtains into the brilliantly lit room beyond.

Captain Shovell's initial impulse was to retreat, pass the cellarman, and trust to finding the right exit before anyone had time to question his presence. Two things arrested him on the point of moving: a sudden vision of his ignominy if he were caught and grappled with by the kitchen knaves, and the sound of his own name loudly spoken in the dining-room.

"Shovell—a silly Norfolk pudding, sir." The voice was harshly contemptuous. "He should be dismissed the service."

"No doubt," rejoined a quieter voice. "Yet I still ask, Sir John—what is in fact being done about him?"

Through the narrow gap between the curtains he could see, by moving his head slightly, the central length of the dining-room. Moorish rugs on a mosaic floor, three gentlemen sitting over their wine at a long table under the great three-tiered candelabrum. He recognized the stout man in blue with a red sash—Sir John Berry, Lord Dartmouth's flag captain—and the little man opposite him wearing a flowered tabby vest under his orange coat, who was the Secretary of the Navy. Beside Mr Pepys sat a big mild-featured gentleman in black brocade, who must be Mr Hodges the merchant-banker. The table was twenty paces from the curtain but the listener could hear every word of a conversation to which he felt bound to listen for more reasons than one. Sir John Berry spoke once more, taking the point further.

"It's near three weeks since the report of this folly with the flags went to Lord Dartmouth, and no action yet. 'S life, Mr Secretary, had I been the admiral I'd have had 'em court-martialled long ago."

Mr Hodges interposed gently. "You forget, Sir John, the companion-in-folly of your Norfolk pudding is the son of an Irish baronet."

"Now, sir—now, Hodges, I can't have that," said Mr Pepys sharply, putting down his wineglass so hastily that the wine spilled over. "A man's birth still sets him high in the Navy whether he be seaman or no—that I'll admit. But from this time forth there shall be no favours because of it, nor shutting of eyes to abuse of the King's service. Moreover, we hope to contrive, and mighty soon, that none but tried seamen command His Majesty's ships."

He drained his glass with a defiant glance at the flag captain. Mr Hodges refilled all three glasses and made a sign to some person outside Clow's field of vision; voices and hurried footsteps beyond the door by which the eavesdropper had come indicated the fetching of more wine.

"I'll drink to that, sir." Berry drank his wine at a draught; he had taken rather more than the others, thought the watcher. "Though you've a labour of Hercules before you, by God! Who's to help you cleanse the Augean stables, ha?"

"The King's brother, Sir John," retorted Mr Pepys.

Sir John hiccuped a laugh. "What? Ninny the great Oof?"

"A moment, gentlemen," Hodges said quickly in a low voice. "My servant, with the wine."

A man in livery placed three bottles on the table and passed from Clow's sight. There was a brief silence broken only by the tinkling of glass and the glucking of poured liquid.

"I'll b-beg His Royal Highness's pardon," said the flag captain magnanimously. "What's more, I'll drink to him. Here's to J-James—and may Charles live for ever!"

Mr Pepys drank half his wine and frowned severely at Berry. His potato-nose was noticeably redder than his plump cheeks.

"Your Lord High Admiral, Sir John," he said in measured and emphatic tones, "to wit, James, Duke of York and Heir Apparent, has the misfortune to be unpopular with the mob and mocked at by those who should know better. This has no pertinence to the fact—and that it is a fact you may be mighty sure, sir—that His Royal Highness has worked vastly harder for the salvation of the Navy than any man before him, king or commoner."

"Oh, fol-de-rol and fiddlestick." Berry splashed wine from a bottle. "We all know what Jamie would do if you gave him the chance, Mr Secretary—a Papist on every quarter-deck and all Protestants overboard."

Mr Pepys, who was drinking, choked indignantly and his face turned as red as his nose. His host put in hurriedly to forestall the angry retort.

"I've had no answer to my question yet. What is to be done about Shovell and Aylmer? And when are we to have an end of this pernicious business of Good Voyages?"

"Th-that's two questions, me boy," giggled Berry, wagging his head so that his wig fell awry.

"Yet are they the same, Sir John, by your leave." The banker-merchant helped Mr Pepys to more wine. "This imbecility of flaunting English colours in Cadiz harbour is but the culmination of many such incidents. I'm loth to say this, Pepys, but in the past twelve months the navy captains in this port have brought the English Navy into contempt with all Spaniards—aye, and with us English merchants too." He paused, his good-humoured face wearing an unwonted scowl. "They toady to the Spanish who may have cargoes for them, insult those who haven't. In order to win a profitable freight— I know of a dozen instances—they'll declare they're bound for such-and-such when in truth they're making in the opposite direction. You may correct me if I'm wrong, Sir John, but I believe the four King's ships that have entered the harbour during the past week are here not on His Majesty's business but on the business they hope to pick up from the Flota when it arrives from the Indies."

"You're right enough." Berry rubbed his chin, hazily doubtful. "Yet it's an old custom, the Good Voyages—I've had a turn at it myself."

"A bad custom for the times, I think," Hodges said quietly. "It's in my mind that a custom that keeps the captains of a Royal Navy ashore for three weeks, swaggering and drinking like Shovell and young Aylmer, leaving our merchant ships to fight alone against the Sallee rovers——"

"Vultures!" shouted Sir John, slapping the table so that the glasses rattled. "Vultures, not navy captains—that's what Shovell and Aylmer are! Shoot 'em, strangle 'em. Why hasn't Dartmouth done it, ha? Mr Shecretary, answer the questions."

It was evident that Mr Pepys was restraining himself with difficulty. He had taken his share of wine and his droll features were heavily flushed. He felt himself the target for his companions' criticisms and showed resentment in the narrow glitter of his little eyes, but he replied quietly and with a careful diction that defied the effects of the wine.

"My Lord Dartmouth will take what action he deems fit, no doubt. It's to be remembered, Sir John, that these two captains are under the command of Admiral Herbert."

"I comprehend you, sir, I comprehend you," Berry said with a sneer. "Admiral Herbert being *p-persona grata* with His Majesty, and a favourite with His Majesty's brother, must not be offended. No favours, you said?"

"You mistake me, Sir John," snapped Mr Pepys angrily. "I intended what you yourself very well know—that Matthew Aylmer and Clowdisley Shovell should be punished, if punishment is due, by their commanding officer."

"Herbert?" Berry guffawed. "If I know Ned Herbert he'll crack a bottle with the lads and say no more. Which reminds me——" He refilled his glass, raised it, then set it down with a sudden access of seriousness. "But you're damned right, Hodges—it's insup—hup—your pardon—insupportable that this breach, that might have lost us our friendship with Spain, should go unpunished. And if Pepys here is afraid to move, by God I'll take it on myself!"

"S-S-Sir John!" stammered Mr Pepys, beetroot-red with wrath. "I must take leave to——"

"I'll write to Lord Dartmouth at Tangier myself," pursued Sir John unheeding. "He's senior to Herbert. He can remove

70

Shovell and Aylmer from their commands, take 'em to England for a full court martial——"

"You may do as you wish," the Secretary interrupted loudly. "But you'd best know, sir, that his lordship received a letter from me at the same time as he received the report of this misdemeanour. In it I requested, with submission, that Captains Aylmer and Shovell should receive no public rebuke or punishment for their folly." He was sitting bolt upright, glaring defiantly at them. Berry choked on his wine and recovered with a gasp.

"D-devil take me if I understand you, Pepys," he blurted. "Why a-God's name must these mountebanks go scot-free?"

"A court martial would end their careers." Mr Pepys looked as though he was beginning to regret his outspokenness. "I care not overmuch in Aylmer's case, but Clowdisley Shovell——"

"What's Shovell that he should be excused?"

"I think, Pepys," said Hodges, frowning, "that having said so much you should explain your—may I say?—unwarrantable action."

The little Secretary hesitated in obvious embarrassment. Then he appeared to come to a difficult resolution. He gulped down his wine, placed both arms on the table, and began to speak in so subdued a tone that the man behind the curtains— now desperately anxious to miss no word—had some difficulty in hearing him.

"I pray you, gentlemen, to hold what I am to say in the closest confidence. If I've exceeded my warrant as Secretary of the Navy, as Mr Hodges has implied, I'm now to exceed it still further. You may be aware—Sir John at least will have heard—that the Navy is to be put into repair, made a fit defence against the new enemy England may have to face."

"To wit, France," grunted Berry. "I hear Louis is building ships at Toulon to the number of——"

"In two years"—Mr Pepys raised his voice—"we shall have

nine first-rates and fifteen second-rates, to name only those. We shall need twenty thousand prime seamen to man them, a hundred sea-officers and twenty-four captains—and the captains must be seamen of the highest merit as well as men courageous, intelligent, loyal to the Navy. Where am I to find such captains, gentlemen? For every John Berry in command today there are twenty incompetents like Carver and Peachell."

"Oh, come, sir," objected Berry, looking pleased nevertheless. "There's John Narbrough, for one."

"Married and ashore, Sir John."

"Well, then—there's young Rooke, John Ashby——"

Berry came to a stop and scratched his head under his wig.

"And Clowdisley Shovell," said Mr Pepys. "Can you add another, on your conscience, that you'd put on the quarter-deck of a King's ship without a qualm of doubt?"

"I'd grant you Shovell," admitted the flag captain, knitting his brows in an effort to overcome the wine-fumes, "were it not for this poxy business of the flags. Shovell can handle a ship with the best in the service."

"And he can handle men, Sir John. I had it in mind that one day I'd see him handle a fleet." The Secretary sighed. "I've kept myself informed upon Clowdisley Shovell. Sir John Narbrough commends him unreservedly, and there was never a better commander than Narbrough. Shovell—so it seemed then—had a conception of ship management and discipline that marched with my own plans for the Navy. I'd hoped—nay, I hope still—to have him on my side in the war I'm waging."

"War?" Berry paused in refilling his glass.

"War, sir. War against place-mongering in the fleet, against drunkenness and incompetence, against rakehelly admirals like Edward Herbert—who will shortly be relieved of his present command if the Board accedes to my request."

"You've asked that Herbert be relieved of command?" The flag captain stared open-mouthed. "You're bold, Pepys—'fore God you're bold!"

Hodges spoke thoughtfully. "It would, I presume, be by Admiral Herbert's orders that these ships came here to wait for cargoes."

Mr Pepys, who had drowned his consciousness of indiscreet talk in another glass, answered him emphatically.

"Precisely so, sir. And it was the captain of the *Charles* who proposed to leave their flags flying to spite the Spaniards—I have it from his second officer. But I don't condone Captain Shovell's folly on these accounts or any other. That he deserves to be punished I admit, Sir John, and freely. But I will not have the Navy robbed of one of the few men who can help me to save it, though I fly in the face of my own rules to keep him from court martial."

Excitement had Mr Pepys in its grip again. His extreme earnestness made his somewhat comical face impressive as he delivered himself of his creed.

"With God's help and the King's, gentlemen, I will frame a great Navy, a Navy of men rather than of ships. Its men shall obey their orders because such is the tradition of this Navy, and they shall do their duty without cavil and in the face of death because they love this Navy and would be ashamed to do otherwise. The King himself shall regulate its ways——"

He was interrupted on the very crest of inspired utterance. Berry got unsteadily to his feet.

"By'r leave, Mr Shecretary," he said thickly. "Regulate myself. Musht pump ship."

Unbuttoning his breeches as he came, he made hurriedly for the retiring-closet.

Captain Shovell had been very much aware of this contingency on his arrival in the closet, but the last few minutes of his eavesdropping had so deeply affected him that he had forgotten his present situation. He was very nearly caught. Had Sir John Berry been sober he must have heard the *clank* as the chamber-pot was kicked a second time and noticed the swinging door on his right as he came through the curtains. As it was, Clow emerged into the dark passage undetected but with his escape yet to be achieved. He had no apprehensions about his next move because it had no place at all in the turmoil of his thoughts, where the Clowdisley Shovell of the past few years was suffering strange mutation; the image he had made of himself was losing its brave colours, like a wax figure cast into seething water, and coming to the surface as a formless thing without design or purpose.

At the end of the passage the Spanish cellarman sat on a low stool with a candle-lanthorn by his side. Clow stalked past the man without a word or look, his sight turned inward. The man scrambled to his feet with a startled *"Madre de Dios!"* stared a moment after him as he crossed the hallway, and then ran to the kitchens. Clow strode on without pause into a passage on the opposite side of the hall. It was unlit but in a dozen paces he came to a door and passed through, heedless of an outburst of voices behind him.

He was out in the night air with the cobbles of the alley underfoot. Starlight, the distant chiming of a bell, nearer at hand the voice of the watch and discordant singing from behind the lit parchment windows of a tavern. He swept off hat and wig, baring his cropped head to the coolness. Mr Pepys's words rang in his mind like an echo of something spoken in the past; they could have been spoken by the Clow Shovell of fifteen years ago. *A great Navy . . . its men shall obey their orders because such is the tradition . . . without cavil and in the face of death . . . and would be ashamed to do otherwise*. The man who said that had saved him from ignominy, too—had counted on him for the making of this Navy of his old vision. By God, Mr Pepys should see that he could still count on Clow Shovell! There should be an end to folly, an end to the shabby creeping after

74

wenches and the drinking-bouts with Aylmer. If Herbert was
to be recalled there would be other changes, and the *James*
might be sent to England. Of its own volition a picture of
Elizabeth Hill rose before him, powdered ringlets caressing
white shoulders, brown eyes smiling kindly. There was the
woman who could stay him from wenching while his devotion
to the Service stayed him from other foolishness. He would
seek her as soon as he landed, begin a courtship——

"Cap'n!" Dick Parr's voice made hoarse interruption.
"Cap'n, sir! Boat's here alongside."

Without knowing how, he had reached the harbour. The
longboat lay at the quay some yards to his left. He stepped
aboard and sat down, silent in the sternsheets.

"Give way, sir?" said Parr.

"Yes—yes. Give way. Put me on board."

The longboat pulled out across the black harbour waters,
its progress demolishing the wavering yellow reflections of
lamplit cabin windows.

"I'll have you pass the word, bo'sun," said Captain Shovell.
"We sail to rejoin the squadron at first light tomorrow."

III

Vice-Admiral Herbert was recalled from his Mediterranean
command as Mr Pepys had urgently requested—but to receive
the mildest of reprimands and be promoted to Rear-Admiral
of England and Commissioner of the Navy. It was whispered
that this was part of the new King's campaign to make favour
with fleet and army officers; for Charles had died in February
of that year, 1685, and his unpopular brother ruled precariously as James the Second. If the Secretary of the Navy felt
the snub, he pursued his own campaign for the cleansing of
the Navy with more vigour than ever. The result, the first
King's Regulation ("in the business of Plate Carriage, etc.,
with his Establishment of an Allowance for their tables and
other encouragements to his Sea-Commanders"), removed

75

once and for all the practice of Good Voyages from naval custom and cleared the way for the establishment of a worthier tradition.

In May of the year that King Charles the Second died, on a morning of blue sky and white clouds with the new leaf green in the hedgerows, Captain Shovell came riding through the woods to the manor-house of Knowlton Court. He had journeyed by coach to Canterbury on the new turnpike road and there hired his mount at the Red Lion Inn. Below the narrow formal garden that flanked the porch was an apple orchard, close on his left as he swung himself from the saddle; and as a fellow came running from the yard to take his horse he saw Elizabeth in the orchard, walking in a yellow sprigged-muslin gown beneath the pink-and-white buds.

"Hold there," he told the groom, and went towards her across the grass.

Her fair ringlets were unpowdered, but otherwise she seemed quite unchanged since he had last seen her, nearly eight years ago.

"Captain Shovell!"

She remembered him, then. Clow, doffing his hat and making a leg with the best grace he could, felt his heart beat faster and cursed himself for an ass.

"Madam, your most devoted. I rejoice to find you among the blossoms—I think myself in the presence of the Queen of the May."

There was little of the Norfolk turnip about Clow Shovell now, but pretty speeches never came easily to him; he was rather pleased with this one. Elizabeth smiled at him—perhaps a little at his ponderous manner, too. Her brown eyes were as kind as he remembered them.

"You've ridden far, sir?" she said. "We'll go into the house and I shall find you some wine. Or perhaps you are ready for food?"

Clow stood firm as she half turned. "I am from London this

morning, and by nightfall must be back again. I come only to deliver a letter, and—and to see you."

He took the packet, silk-tied and sealed, from the breast of his tunic and held it out to her. She took it, keeping her eyes on his round face, hard and brown from his voyaging.

"I had the honour to dine with Sir John in London," Clow explained. "He asked me to bring you the letter, with his duty."

"But you'll stay a while, Captain Shovell?" she pleaded. "It's long since we met, though Sir John has very often talked of you. It is still 'captain', isn't it?"

"Still 'captain'," he admitted with a faint smile. "But I cannot stay—it's five hours to London and I must keep an appointment there at seven o'clock."

His appointment was not until tomorrow. But he had firmly resolved to leave at once when he had seen her; the disappointment coming after long months of hope still rankled.

"If it's a lady," said Elizabeth smiling, "you were wise not to keep her waiting."

The hint of a question in her tone pleased and pained him both together.

"I'm to present myself at the Navy Office," he told her. "I have it from Sir John, in confidence, that I'm to be given a ship. A second-rater, seventy guns."

"I felicitate you with all my heart, Captain," she said with a warmth that was not feigned. "The ship could not have a worthier captain."

Captain Shovell was embarrassed and spoke quickly to cover it. "I've felicitations to proffer too, I fear very tardily. Allow me, Lady Narbrough, to—to felicitate you, and your most fortunate husband."

"It is indeed somewhat late," Elizabeth said gently. "I've been married nearly four years. But I thank you just as heartily."

"You'll understand, I—I trust, madam, that news is slow

77

to reach a squadron on service. I heard yours only when I came ashore in Spithead. And I have it from Sir John that you've a—a family."

"A girl and a boy." She gestured towards the house. "Will you see them?"

"I cannot, madam. I must take my leave, and at once."

"So soon?" The brown eyes that regarded him so steadily were sad. "I see I can't detain you. But you'll visit Knowlton before you sail, I hope, and stay longer."

"I fear it will be impossible, madam." It was impossible that he should see her again, knowing as he did that he loved her. "There's much to do and little time for it. And so—farewell."

He took the hand she held to him and kissed it, then walked swiftly across the orchard grass to his horse.

"God-speed, Captain!" Elizabeth called to him.

Captain Shovell threw his booted leg over the saddle, turned to wave his hat, and kicked his mount into motion. Lady Narbrough ran to the orchard's edge where she could watch until he passed from sight among the trees of the park. Clow was not the sort of horseman whom it is a pleasure to watch, nor did he once turn his head; but she stood with her gaze on the big jogging figure as long as she could see it, and remained there gazing at nothing for some minutes afterwards. In her hand was her husband's letter, unopened.

FOUR

Captain Clowdisley Shovell stood alone on *Dover*'s quarter-deck in the windy October night. Above him the great stern-lantern winked and flickered with the north-easterly gusts, beneath his feet the deck planking shuddered under the cease-less hammering of the short steep sea. Every half-minute or so there was a jerk and a jarring of spar and hawser as *Dover*'s anchor-cable came taut, causing Captain Shovell to make a sort of dancing step for the retention of his balance and to mutter an irritable curse. The repetitive swearing did a little to relieve his temper, which was—with some reason—unusually bad.

Looking out to larboard from his quarter-deck rail he could see a galaxy of yellow stars, the lights of the fleet. Fifty ships lay anchored off the Essex coast to oppose the invasion of Dutch William, and not one of them a first- or second-rate fighting ship. The twenty-one strongest vessels of King James's Navy were all either refitting or under repair, his own *Anne*, the 70-gun ship he had been appointed to command, among them, and this at a time of crisis such as had not been seen since the Armada. Muddle and disorder once again, when the Navy had seemed on the point of becoming the Service that Mr Pepys had striven to make it. Captain Shovell knew now that the Secretary for the Affairs of the Admiralty (which was Mr Pepys's new title) was not responsible; responsibility lay wholly with the King.

Clow's father, a yeoman of some little fortune, had paid a crippling forfeit to the Commonwealth government for his loyalty to King Charles the First. But if his son had any lingering belief in divine right it had been dispelled by the behaviour of King James, who had proved himself a very fool and Mr Pepys a shocking bad prophet. *A Papist on every quarter-deck and all Protestants overboard*—for an instant he was back in the retiring-closet at Cadiz as he recalled Sir John Berry's words. It was what the King had attempted so soon as he came to power. Mass to be heard in all ships—but it was the priests who went overboard when the seamen got the chance to do it. And the ships he had once cared for left to rot while the King spent the last penny of his revenue on raising an army of Irish Catholics to oppose his English army, which had turned mutinous because he insisted on replacing all Protestant officers with Papists. Pah! (Clow spat over the rail, there being no one to see him.) A fool of fools, deserving to lose his crown, as he was like to do. Yet—he was the King, and Clowdisley Shovell captained a King's ship.

He pulled his boat-cloak closer about him against the chill wind and strained his ears for the sound of oars coming from larboard. *Dover* lay on the fringe of the anchored fleet and in the rear, half a mile away from Lord Dartmouth's flagship; which was why (he supposed) she had been chosen for the meeting, the Admiral having ordered all captains to remain on board their ships. These cabals and secret meetings had been going on for weeks—nay, months—and Captain Shovell hated them. If the message hadn't come from Vice-Admiral Sir John Berry himself he'd have refused to make *Dover* a rendezvous for sedition. A stronger gust of the north-easter brought to his ears the moaning of seas on the Gunfleet shoal. When it had died he heard plainly the creak and splash of approaching boats, and went to the taffrail to call to the cluster of dark figures by the mainmast.

"Entry port, bo'sun."

"Aye aye, sir."

The hoarse reply momentarily turned Clow's thoughts from

the coming meeting. That double *aye* in response to an order seemed to be spreading from ship to ship; he had noticed its use on board Captain Tennant's *Tiger*, and now here it was in the mouth of Dick Parr. Another thing (he meditated as he went down to the stern cabin) was this about the larboard side. The entry port in a warship was always on the larboard side giving on to the main deck, with a fixed ladder of steps leading up to it, and the growing tendency to refer to this flank as "the port side" was natural enough. It might be a good thing if the term became general. There was a likeness about the sounds of "larboard" and "starboard" that he had found awkward before now when orders had to be shouted against half a gale.

He had reached the cabin and it was no longer possible to escape the impending conclave by thinking of other things. The low-beamed space, twenty-five feet by fifteen, looked poky by the light of the lamp that swung from the deckhead, but it would have to serve for the score or more of captains that might be expected. Sea-chests and empty casks had been brought in to supplement the few chairs round the central table, which was bolted irremovably to the deck. Wine there was none. Even if Clow had been able to afford it on ten pounds a month, which he could not, he would have declined to give wine to men who came on board to plot (as he assumed) against their commanding officer.

An irregular dull thudding and the trampling of boots heralded the first-arrivals and Captain Shovell went to the cabin door to receive them. With a vice-admiral coming on board, he should have been at the entry port or at least on deck, but he was stubborn enough to pay no respect where he felt respect was not due. Sir John Berry's scowl as he came in flinging off his boat-cloak was conceivably on account of this lack of ceremony. Half a dozen captains followed him, among them Ashby of the *Defiant* and his old companion of Mediterranean days, Matt Aylmer, who had the *Swallow*, 48. There had been a coolness between Matt and himself since he had sailed the *James* back from Cadiz, and the intervening four years had seen few meetings between them and those occasioned only by duty. Greetings were terse and no one was inclined to talk. By the time Captain Shovell had seated the stout vice-admiral in the central chair at the table and invited the rest to sit where they pleased, another batch of officers was coming in. They brought the number of guests to seventeen. After a few minutes of uneasy waiting Sir John announced peevishly that he proposed to begin.

"Nothing that's said in this cabin goes out of it, through me or anyone else," he said without further preamble. "Every man here is on oath of honour in this respect. You may withdraw if you wish."

No one spoke. Berry nodded satisfaction.

"And we'll have no ceremony. Captain Shovell's set us an example there."

He darted a malicious glance at *Dover*'s captain, who was seated on an upturned cask wearing the expression of imperturbable gravity he was lately accustomed to assume. Matt Aylmer risked a wink from the vice-admiral's blind side and received the flutter of an eyelid in return; whereby it was conceded on both sides that old comradeship was not forgotten.

"You'll wish to know why you're here, gentlemen," Berry went on, and was interrupted at once.

"We wish to know why the fleet's here, Sir John," said Tennant of the *Tiger*.

A growl of assent came from half a dozen others. Berry glared but remembered in time his renunciation of ceremony.

"Very well," he said curtly. "The fleet's here in the lee of the Gunfleet, where it's been a month too long, because Admiral Lord Dartmouth don't want to put to sea. I dare say you know why as well as I do. His lordship's a favourite of King James and his Admiral of the Fleet, but Papist or no he's had enough of James."

"So have we all," said Captain Ashby loudly.

" 'S life, will you let me speak?" Berry snapped. "So Dartmouth's playing to lose, that's clear. The Admiralty, as they call themselves now, ordered him to take the fleet off Helvetsluys a month ago. If he'd done it, the Prince of Orange would have lost his labour of ships and transports and guns for invasion of England. But no—my lord can't move for lack of victuals, or winds, or tides, or what you will. It's the same now. Pepys and his gang shove the Admiral's rump until he has to move, so he brings us down to the Gunfleet."

"A damned foul anchorage," said someone.

"As he well knows," retorted Sir John. "The wind can blow from twenty-four points of the compass and hold us weatherbound. With this Protestant wind blowing the admiral can't put so much as a frigate in William's way, were he to sail with all his Dutchmen—and his English troops—tomorrow, as well he might. So. What do you gentlemen think of the situation you're in?"

The assembled captains looked at each other; some scratched their heads, some grinned. Captain Ashby spoke up.

"I'd say it suits most of us very well," he said boldly. "Fo'c's'le and quarter-deck, there's not one-third of this fleet wouldn't rather welcome Dutch William than fight him."

"And that", put in Captain Williams of the *St Albans*, "shows the Navy lagging behind the rest of England, look you. In the west every man is whistling 'Lilliburlero', and in Cardiff this 5th November they'll have James on the bonfires 'stead of Guido Fawkes."

Captain Shovell spoke from his cask-seat in a corner. "We were to hear why we are gathered here, Sir John."

"My thanks for the reminder, Captain Shovell," said Berry sarcastically; he looked round his audience. "You're here because I don't know your minds, gentlemen. I've had some conversation with the other captains of this fleet and all but a very few are of the same mind as myself."

83

"And we are now to know that mind, sir?" inquired Captain Aylmer with suspicious innocence.

Sir John answered obliquely. "You all know of my past quarrel with Admiral Herbert, no doubt. On June the twenty-ninth of this year Admiral Herbert showed himself a man of greater sense and courage than I am."

Again the captains exchanged glances. June 29th was the date (everyone knew it now) when Edward Herbert had crossed to Holland with an invitation to William, husband of James's eldest daughter, to come to England and claim the throne. It was Herbert who held supreme command of the Dutch invasion forces, with the rank of Lieutenant-Admiral-General.

"If you're minded to see King William on the throne, sir," said Captain Tennant cautiously, "as it may be we are also, should we not be content with Lord Dartmouth's present—um—inaction?"

Sir John slammed his open hand on the table. "No, by God!" he declared forcibly. "For what are we in William's eyes? Enemies under arms to oppose him, yet dallying cowardly and unseamanlike behind the Gunfleet to save our skins. The man's a soldier and a great fighter. If he comes to the throne——"

"God send he does!" a voice interjected.

"—d'you think he'll ask fellows of that kidney to command ships in the King's Navy? Devil take me if I think so!"

"Therefore you have something to propose, sir," said Captain Shovell.

The vice-admiral glanced askance at Shovell's round expressionless face and turned his shoulder to him.

"I'm a plain seaman and no politician, gentlemen," he said bluffly. "I'll put it short and clear. I'm for William of Orange and I propose to tell him so. I propose to sail as soon as I can leave the Gunfleet, with such ships as will follow me, and join Prince William's force off the Maas. Who's with me?"

Five or six of those present shouted "I!" at once; as many others followed after some hesitation. John Ashby of the *Defiant*, a hard-featured man of proven courage and seamanship, rubbed his square chin in frank puzzlement.

"I'm not one that would go against his admiral, Sir John," he said slowly, "and yet I'd not see a Catholic succession. 'Twould be the end of England. Your way of it looks to be the honest way——"

"It looks to be mutiny and treason," Captain Aylmer broke in harshly.

Berry turned his ponderous form deliberately, facing Aylmer. Captain Shovell expected a furious outburst, but the vice-admiral's reply was made in a quieter tone than he had yet used.

"You'd call me a traitor, Captain Aylmer. Very well—but you must also apply that name to the Duke of Ormonde, the Duke of Grafton, my Lord Cornbury, my Lord Churchill— aye, and to Lord Edward Russell, once of the King's Navy and now at Orange's right hand. And to some hundreds of thousands of Englishmen beside. The very Catholics of James's household have deserted him. If this fleet fights the Dutch, it'll be fighting for a few Papists whose fortunes sink or swim with the Stuarts." He changed the direction of his glance suddenly. "And what has Captain Clowdisley Shovell to say to that?"

Clow's answer came unhurriedly but without hesitation. He had debated this matter long ago, and with much searching of his heart had come to a firm decision.

"I say, Sir John," he said, with a touch of broad Norfolk in his utterance, "that I'm captain of a King's ship and my loyalty's to my admiral in command."

"But God's life, man, where's Lord Dartmouth's loyalty?" cried Sir John testily. "He's making sure he don't have a chance of opposing the Prince of Orange."

"There can be two opinions as to that, sir." It seemed almost as if Captain Shovell was purposely using the slow drawl of the country yokel. "It's true Lord Dartmouth shows as if he's dwindlin' about here, but there's many would hold he's prudent not to take his ships to sea at October-end, in the weather we're having. To continue"—he held up a large fore-finger to prevent Berry's interruption—"the admiral's loyalty say I, is to the King. The King's loyalty is to England. Now, if the King breaks his loyalty—as seems to me he has broken it—that's no reason why I should break mine. That's how I see my duty, Sir John. And I ha' done."

The vice-admiral swung away from him with angry impatience.

"God save us from fools!" he said. "Most of you gentlemen, I'm glad to know, see that your duty and loyalty lie with the Prince who can save your country. Mark ye, now. You and your ships, joined to the others who've seen sense, make up a good three dozen. My ensign at the mizzen yard-arm is the signal for weighing. If the admiral don't sail at the first change of wind, that signal flies and you'll follow me out."

"And if we're fired on?" asked Captain Williams doubt-fully.

Sir John snorted. "Captain Shovell and Captain Aylmer have my leave to try it. If they find one gun-crew willing to load, I'll turn Papist." He stood up abruptly. "That's all. I'll venture to remind every gentleman here that he's bound by oath to secrecy."

He marched out, taking up his boat-cloak as he went, and the captains filed from the cabin behind him. Aylmer lingered to grip Clow's hand briefly; then the captain of the *Dover* had his stern-cabin to himself.

Captain Shovell allowed the conspirators time to get clear of his ship's side before summoning the watch-on-deck to put the cabin to rights and send his first lieutenant, Tyldesley, to him. All his officers had been ordered to keep to their cabins while the conference was in progress. To Tyldesley he gave the routine orders for the anchor watch, with a reminder of the admiral's instruction that a lookout was to be kept at *Dover*'s masthead from first light onwards; her position in the anchored fleet gave his ship the best opportunity of descrying any movement of shipping on the eastward horizon. This done, he turned in and slept soundly. He had no doubts about the stand he had taken; it was both his strength and his weakness that he never reconsidered a decision once it was made. As for the problem of action when the vice-admiral fulfilled his intention of deserting, that could be faced when it arose . . .

The problem never did arise. Chance, or destiny, enabled Admiral Lord Dartmouth to do his duty in the service of King James without interfering in the triumph of Prince William.

On the third day after the conference in *Dover*'s cabin, which was the 1st November, the look-out at her masthead sighted a large fleet moving southward through the haze that lay across the waters east of the Gunfleet. The admiral ordered all ships to weigh and proceed in chase, despite the fact that the fitful breeze still backed and veered between north-east and south-east. For two days his fifty vessels beat back and forth, trying to win clear of the Galloper and the Gabbard and every shoal and sand between Harwich and the Kentish Knock, and when at last they passed the Straits it was only to lie becalmed off Beachy Head while William, landing in Torbay, was welcomed with shouts of "A free Parliament and the Protestant religion!"

So the power and dominion of England changed hands without a fight. By the time Admiral of the Fleet Lord Dartmouth had made submission with all his fleet to King William, James Stuart was already in France with Louis XIV, planning the counter-revolution—an invasion from Ireland with French ships and troops aiding an army of Catholic Irish. Clowdisley Shovell, appointed to command the *Edgar*, 64, learned that he was to serve under Admiral Edward Herbert, whom he despised, against the royal exile who had once been Mr Pepys's most powerful ally in the shaping of the new Navy.

As for Mr Samuel Pepys, his work for the Navy was finished. King William accepted without reluctance the resignation of the Secretary for the Affairs of the Admiralty; and his friend John Evelyn wrote the finis for him: "He laid down his office and would serve no more."

II

"They're hauling their wind, sir," said Lieutenant Purvis. "They'll not play our game."

"It was to be expected." Captain Shovell's tone, like his face, evinced a placidity he was far from feeling. "Flagship's wearing, Mr Purvis. Stand by to wear ship," he added over his shoulder to the two helmsmen.

"Bra-a-aces!" yelled Purvis from the taffrail.

The main courses shivered and flapped, the canvas of the driver cracked like a whiplash as the *Edgar*'s massive stern swung slowly round to bring the wind on the starboard quarter. With the gradual swing of the ship the low green shape of Dursey Island crawled across the grey water to lie on the starboard beam. The French fleet, twenty-five of the line, made a long row of white oblongs in front of the island and the mainland cape of Crow Head, a row that was moving slowly back towards the entrance of Bantry Bay whence they had come. Shovell looked to where *Diamond* surged and wallowed on his larboard side, almost within hail. On his other side Ashby's *Defiant* was turning towards the wind—the admiral was once again going to beat up towards the enemy, it seemed.

"Bear up," he growled at the quartermasters. "Look alive, Mr Purvis. Braces."

Purvis was far too fond of gazing through his telescope. If he'd keep his glass trained on the *Elizabeth* it might be some use; but when, as now, the flagship was obscured by the hull and towering canvas of his next-in-line the only thing to do was to watch your neighbours and follow their actions. A poor system and needing amendment. Herbert, behindhand in this as in much else, had issued no code of signals, though he had sent his battle orders to all ships while they had been lying-to in the offing last night—last night, when the battle should have been over and done with.

Course was being altered again, towards the wind. *Edgar*'s yards were braced to a beam wind now, and the manœuvre brought the nineteen English ships in line ahead with George Churchill's *Pendennis* leading, the flagship in the centre, and *Diamond*—just astern of *Edgar*—last in the line as it made towards the extended French fleet. The French, still close-hauled, continued to move across the five-mile-wide entrance of Bantry Bay towards the point of Muntervary. Long before Herbert could come within gunshot they would be dead to windward again. Captain Shovell stared ahead into the moist easterly breeze and sighed for opportunity lost.

He knew, as did every captain in the fleet, that the admiral's task had been to intercept the French and prevent them from landing troops—some said 10,000 men, but it was more likely to be 5,000—to support James Stuart. In Captain Shovell's view it was a highly important task. There was officially no war between France and England. It was the more urgent, therefore, to demonstrate once for all that this landing of soldiers to attack from Ireland (it was the first time such a thing had been tried) could be prevented. The offenders should be chastised, of course—but the prevention was the vital thing. And what had happened? Herbert had been given the chance and had thrown it away. After cruising since mid April off Cork and Brest and in the Channel mouth, he had sighted the French fleet on the evening of April 30th, beating against an easterly—no usual wind on the coast of Cork—into Bantry Bay. Herbert could have engaged before they passed Crow Head. Instead, he had drawn back to lie all night in the offing, while the French had no doubt worked furiously at the disembarking of stores and soldiers, completing their own task successfully.

It had been approaching dusk when the French fleet was sighted; true. No fleet commander willingly began a sea-fight that might continue into hours of darkness; true. But a seaman with some imagination would have realized (as Captain Shovell had realized) how vulnerable were those deep-laden French ships, their decks cluttered with military equipment and their 'tween-decks encumbered with soldiers, most of them probably seasick. A swift and resolute attack had had an excellent chance of doing Herbert's business—but it had been a chance, and he would not take it. Instead, he had taken his ships into the bay next morning as soon as it was light; to windward, into a narrowing inlet where there was no room to manœuvre and the enemy had the weather gage from the start. The necessity of repeated tacking had naturally disorganized the English battle-line completely, and the French, coming easily down on them from windward to engage at halfpast ten, had inflicted a certain amount of damage before Herbert comprehended his fatal disadvantage and took all his ships out to sea again.

In that brief but disastrous engagement *Edgar* had borne no active part, for she had been in the rear and the retreat had begun before she could come to quarters with a Frenchman. Now, at halfpast two in the afternoon, Captain Shovell was beginning to wonder if his gun-crews—at ease in their little groups round the upper-deck guns—would ever get a chance to fire their weapons. The French had come out of the bay, but Châteaurenault, their admiral, was evidently seaman enough to defeat all Herbert's efforts to get to windward of him.

"I think they're altering course, sir," said the first lieutenant at his elbow, peering through the unnecessary telescope. "I think they're going about to meet us."

"I think so too," returned Captain Shovell. "Shorten that

instrument of yours, Mr Purvis. Place it in the skirt pocket of your coat. And please to see that all upper-deck guns are in readiness—matches alight, water-buckets full, powder and shot at hand."

"Certainly, sir." Purvis turned to go to the ladder.

" 'Aye aye, sir,' on board my ship, Mr Purvis. And pass the word for Mr Friend and the sailing-master."

"Cert—aye aye, sir."

The crews of the after guns a few feet for'ard of the quarter-deck ladder had plainly overheard that conversation. They were up on their horny bare feet, spitting on their hands and grinning like lunatics at the prospect of blowing Frenchmen to pieces—or of being blown to pieces themselves. Or perhaps (reflected Shovell) they were merely sick and tired of endless gun-drill with empty pieces and rejoiced at the chance of making a lusty bang with real powder and a real ball. The weeks of searching for the French had given him a fair knowledge of his ship's company, though he had been in command of *Edgar* for less than three months. Of his 470 hands, about half could be called seamen and half of those prime seamen; the rest were a mixture of inexperienced volunteers, pressed men, gaolbirds and invalids. According to what he had heard of *Defiant*'s crew, he was more fortunate than John Ashby. He had competent men in the warrant ranks—gunner, carpenter, boatswain; a lucky chance had enabled him to transfer Dick Parr from *Dover* as his boatswain. Godfrey the aged sailing-master knew his business, and so did Friend, his second lieutenant, while Purvis, though an ass in some things, had nothing to learn about a first lieutenant's job of keeping the hands hard at it. All in all, he commanded a vessel as efficient and well-found as any third-rater in the Service (there were no first- or second-rate ships in Herbert's fleet) and he was confident that *Edgar* would give a good account of herself in a fight—if she got the chance.

And it looked as if she was going to get that chance. This

time the admiral appeared to be holding on towards the enemy instead of repeating yet again that futile stratagem.

"Ah, Mr Friend"—the second lieutenant had come up on the quarter-deck—"we may be in action shortly. You will of course command the main-deck guns. I want the starboard broadside ready to fire and the larboard guns standing by. See to it, if you please."

"Aye aye, sir." Friend had learned his captain's peculiar whim more quickly than Purvis. "Skeleton crews for the larboard guns?"

"Yes. Three men. If we come to close quarters I'll send down extra hands."

This was a major problem of the Navy, Clow meditated, as Mr Friend, having touched his triple-cocked hat, departed. There could never be enough hands to man all a ship's guns without reducing the number necessary to work a ship under full sail. *Edgar* carried twenty-four demi-cannon on her lower deck, 32-pounders with a crew of six men; the thirty-six 12-pounders on her upper deck, poop and forecastle required four men to each gun, and the long 4-pounders mounted in pairs as bow-chasers and stern-chasers required three. Three hundred men; and the shot-handlers, powder-monkeys, loblolly boys and musket-men made another hundred. That left seventy hands for the multitude of tasks involved in handling the ship —making or taking in sail (and there were thirteen sails when she was carrying all her canvas) manning the halyards and braces, steering, look-outs, cooks. A bigger ship with more hands meant more and bigger guns. The 42-pounders on the first-rates needed a crew of eight. So you could fight one broadside and keep your sails, or reduce your canvas to a minimum for ease of handling and thus keep your guns manned. The solution? Fewer and more efficient guns, perhaps. Or——

"Sir?"

The sailing-master was at his side.

"Take station here, Mr Capstick. Should it come to a general action I wish to give my attention to the upper-deck guns."

Before he had finished speaking there came the squeal of a trumpet, faint but clear, from the flagship, followed instantly by a *rafale* of drums which swelled and came nearer as ship after ship took it up. Purvis's roar of "Beat to quarters, there!" was belated, but the drummer was ready. To the surging roll of the drum *Edgar*'s crew went to their action stations, while their captain watched keenly from his quarter-deck taffrail. For this was a drill instituted by Captain Shovell, in accordance with his desire that all things should be orderly done. Groups of men mustered under appointed leaders and hastened in silence to their places; the musketeers filed up to the poop with their weapons properly held and stood in rank, at ease; the gun-crews grouped themselves precisely round their guns, loader and rammer, swabber and hauliers. The ship's boy detailed to act as captain's messenger (as Clow had been—how long ago? Twenty-three years, God ha' mercy!) trotted nimbly up to the quarter-deck to stand well out of the way. And here came Lieutenant Purvis at a jogtrot, sweating slightly, to report, according to his instructions, that all was in order and ready for action.

It was very well. But Captain Shovell allowed no trace of his pleasure to appear on his large round face; a disciple of Narbrough in this as in many other things, he considered it the part of a Navy captain to preserve his imperturbability in every circumstance. He touched his hat to Purvis's salute and bade him to take up his own station on the fore-deck. It was delightful to note, while he was doing this, that the noise and chatter of *Defiant*'s crew going to quarters was still audible ahead of *Edgar*. A fine seaman, John Ashby, and a born fighter, but much inclined to be slapdash.

The French fleet, or what he could see of it beyond the huge curving edge of the mainsail, looked very little nearer than before; they were rather less than a mile and a half distant, he judged, moving almost imperceptibly on a course west-sou'-west or thereabouts. Herbert had set his ships beating to quarters long before it was needed, for with this wind, too gentle to break the surface of the long grey-green swell, it would be twenty minutes or more before they came within the longest gunshot of the enemy. But Herbert, of course, must be in a right tissic (reflected Clow with an inward grin) finding himself England's champion at sea. The foul-mouthed adventurer of the Tangier squadron might well be regretting the bold stroke by which he had won William's favour and trust, now that so much depended on his leadership of his country's only fleet. Already he had lost half the battle by his shuffling. Only by soundly drubbing the French, showing Louis that France had no hope of keeping open her communications with Ireland, could he claim to have achieved anything. Middleton, his flag-captain in *Elizabeth*, was a sound adviser; but Herbert was as opinionated as he was inefficient.

The thought of the flagship's name swung his contemplations to another Elizabeth. Lady Narbrough had been lonely at Knowlton Court for some time, though she had a third child, a boy, to comfort her now. Sir John had sailed for Barbados eighteen months ago at Albemarle's request, to salvage treasure from a sunken galleon, it was said. Did she weep often for her absent husband, he wondered? Did she ever give a thought to the man she had seen on two occasions only, who——

"*Pendennis* is wearing, sir!" said Capstick urgently.

The fair brown-eyed face vanished, its place taken by sea and sky and the far line of enemy sail. Across the mid distance of the scene, emerging from behind the obscuring curve of *Edgar*'s mainsail, came *Pendennis*. Astern of her *Mary* came into sight (that was Matt Aylmer's ship) and both were furling their lower sails. Herbert was wearing his fleet in line parallel with the French line—and the distance between the two fleets was still scarcely less than a mile. The fool!

"Mr Purvis!" The men at quarters were so quiet that his bellow sounded unnecessarily loud. "Stand by to take in sail —main courses and spritsails! Hands to the braces!"

One by one the great ships wore to larboard as they reached *Pendennis*'s turning-point. The French and English lines were now moving slowly on the same course, south-west, with the wind on their larboard quarter and a little more than three-quarters of a mile between the two fleets. What in the devil's name did Herbert hope to gain by this? The French wouldn't close; their only object now was to keep their ships intact, and if they could do that their triumph would be complete. If the admiral intended a damaging action he should have made his turn when the fleets were within half-gunshot at the farthest. Then these starboard broadsides could have done some mischief. As it was, there'd be a hit-or-miss game of dropping shots at a range of seven cable-lengths—if it was proposed to open fire at all.

"See there!"

The sailing-master's exclamation and pointing finger drew his attention. One of the French ships, towards the rear of the line fronting them across the glassy expanse of heaving water, had vanished in a mushroom of smoke lit by orange flames. The roar of the explosion reached him as he saw it.

"Blown up, by God!" declared Capstick. "None of our——"

"Mr Bream!" Shovell called to the gunner on the upper deck. "Your target's the third ship to the left of that blaze. Are your quoins in?"

"Yessir—full elevation, sir."

"Take them back an inch. Range fourteen hundred yards. Fire when I wave my hat, and not before. Boy! did you hear me give the target?"

"Yes, sir—third ship to the left of the blaze."

"Good. Repeat that to Mr Friend on the lower deck, with my compliments. Fast as you can go."

He turned to stare at the enemy as the boy leapt down the

quarter-deck ladder. The damaged French ship, a fourth-rater by the look of her, had drifted wide of the line and the ships astern of her were losing their stations. Whatever the cause of the explosion (a chance spark in the ready-use ammunition was the likeliest) it would probably shock the French into opening fire. His surmise was proved correct within one minute. A Frenchman in the centre of the line, the flagship judging by the enormous white-and-gold flags at her stern and mainmast, disappeared behind the smoke of her larboard broadside, and almost at once the firing was taken up all along the mile-and-a-half of enemy vessels.

"Stand by, Mr Bream."

And there went *Elizabeth*'s broadside. Shovell waved his hat, and *Edgar* reeled and shuddered to the deafening explosion, which was followed instantly by a second shattering roar as the lower-deck guns went off. Not perfect unison in either case, but very creditable all the same, thought Shovell with his glass to his eye.

"Stop vents!" Bream was yelling. "Shove those bloody swabs right down the barrel. Reload, run out, and wait the word."

The hazy round of the lens showed *Edgar*'s target, a ship of about her own force, gliding calmly on the gentle swell, but he could neither make out the splashes of his falling shot nor discern any damage they might have done.

"The monseers are firing high, sir," commented the sailing-master. "The balls passed——"

The din of *Defiant*'s and *Diamond*'s broadsides firing simultaneously drowned his words. John Ashby and Walters needed to smarten up a bit; twenty seconds behind *Edgar*.

"Elevation down a morsel, Mr Bream," Shovell called.

The lower-deck guns went off a second after he spoke. Friend could be trusted to see those guns didn't fire wildly. Shovell waved his hat again to the watchful Bream and trained his glass on the enemy as the guns roared out. A splash or two dead in line with the target—but *Edgar* had rolled to starboard as they fired. No use in altering elevation again; the varied imperfections of guns and powder and balls made it ridiculous to try for accuracy at this range. Fire on, hit or miss.

"Mr Bream! Broadsides in your own time."

And now the cannonade was nearly continuous, a broken rhythm of violent explosions with an irregular echo from across the water. Shovell could soon see other ships of the English fleet besides *Defiant* and *Diamond*, for their station-keeping had as usual been upset by the repeated firing of broadsides, but he could see no sign of damage among them. What glimpses he had of the French through the drifting cannon-smoke were of ships busily firing and apparently untouched. Clow so far forgot the imperturbable Captain Shovell as to slam his big fist into his palm and swear under his breath. If only he could have two minutes with the admiral! He'd persuade him somehow—with a cudgel if all else failed—that his only course was to close the French. If Herbert couldn't see that the credit of the English Navy was in the balance at this moment, he could at least be made to realize that the reputation of Edward Herbert was in an equally precarious state.

Ten minutes. Twenty, and they were still banging uselessly away at each other. Not quite without effect, though—he caught sight of a topmast falling in a tangle of canvas and cordage beyond his next ahead; that would be Captain Delavall's *York*. With so much shot thickening the air a lucky hit was bound to come. And as the thought came into his mind there was a multiple screeching in the air overhead and a hole appeared as if by magic in the mizzen topsail. He caught sight of the messenger, close behind him, straightening his ducked head with a sheepish grin.

The guns on the upper deck were firing to Bream's order, almost leisurely, waiting the clearing of the smoke which always took longer with a following breeze. The breeze was freshening now—but not so much, surely, that it could deaden

G 97

the noise of *Defiant*'s guns? No! *Defiant* had ceased firing. And Purvis, high up in the bows, was screeching and waving frantically.

"Hard a-larboard!" yelled Capstick behind him.

Edgar began to swing round, her beakhead threatening to shave the gilded ornamentation from *Defiant*'s stern as it passed across her bows. For Ashby's ship had turned to starboard out of the line, heading towards the French; and there was Ashby himself at the rail, waving his hat and shouting something about rudder-cables damaged. He was near enough as the two ships sheered past each other for the broad grin on his face to be evident. He made beckoning gestures with his hat as *Defiant* drew clear. Damaged rudder-cables—no court martial would accept that excuse. So be damned to excuses!

"Starboard helm, there!" snapped Clow. "I'm wearing ship." And to the messenger—"Lower deck, quick. My order to Mr Friend—cease fire." He jumped to the after-deck. "Cease fire, all guns cease fire! Man the weather braces, there —meet her, Mr Capstick—steady! Haul, haul—make fast!"

Edgar had come right round, past her original course, and was heading after *Defiant* with the freshening breeze just abaft the beam from starboard. There was actually a smile on Clow's big round face; until Captain Shovell the disciplinarian returned to remind him that he was acting without orders and against the plain policy of his commanding officer in thus imitating the ingenious Captain Ashby. Well, better to hang with Ashby than hide behind a disgraced Herbert.

"I want both broadsides manned and ready, Mr Bream. Send a hand down to Mr Friend with that order."

This was *Edgar*'s best point of sailing and she was fast covering the half-mile that would bring her to close gunshot. Four lengths ahead was *Defiant*, on his larboard bow. As he glanced at her he saw a dozen rents appear in her canvas and a large piece of timber—part of her upper-deck bulwarks—hurtle into the sea. She was heading straight for the French flagship.

"Starboard a point. Steady as you go."

He was bringing *Edgar* into the gap between the two Frenchmen lying second and third from the flagship, so that he could use both broadsides. The din of the French broadsides grew louder, right ahead. A screaming of balls, a crash above and very near, and the mizzen yard dropped like a headsman's axe, missing him by six feet but smashing into the rank of musketeers on the poop, killing one outright and injuring another who lay screaming. Dick Parr headed the little party that ran up to clear the wreckage, but Captain Shovell had no glance for them as they hauled the splintered wood and broken human flesh out of the way. He had time for a glance astern, to see that at least four ships (one of them was Matt Aylmer's *Mary*) had left the English line and were coming in to engage closely. Then, as the crash of *Defiant*'s guns came to his ears, he turned to see the red-painted side of a French ship a hundred yards ahead of his bowsprit. A second afterwards the red-painted side vomited flame and smoke and immediately Captain Shovell was lying on the quarter-deck kicking his legs and trying to regain his breath. The French broadside that swept *Edgar*'s upper deck from bow to stern had passed above the waist without touching the masts and had vented most of its force on the high poop and quarter-deck, blasting two ragged gaps in the rail and sending a round wooden moulding from the balusters to wind Captain Shovell. He was on his feet now, clutching bruised ribs, glancing swiftly round him: Capstick a twitching headless corpse, half the after-rail gone and one of the helmsmen with it, the remaining helmsman with blood all over his face from a splinter-wound but still clutching the spokes of the wheel. Shovell sprang to the other side of the wheel.

"Starboard—hard over!"

Edgar had been on the point of ramming her beakhead into the Frenchman's quarter. She sheered away, passing so close that Shovell had an instantaneous picture of a pistol aimed at him from twenty feet away by a sallow-faced man on the enemy's quarter-deck. Hat and wig were twitched from his head as the pistol exploded. The muskets up on his own poop-deck were banging away at short range.

"Larboard, now—steady!"

Edgar, swinging to the helm, drove across the Frenchman's wake. As she did so her larboard guns fired as they bore, every shot from thirty cannon crashing into the carved and gilded stern from a range of half a pistol-shot. At the same time her starboard broadside thundered, hurling five hundredweight of iron into the bows and along the deck of the next ship in the line.

The cannonade ceased abruptly. She was through the French line with the beam wind still urging her on. Two hands came leaping up to take over the wheel, others dealt with Capstick's body and the wounded helmsman. Now he could pick up his wig and jam it on—of his hat there was no sign. Bream was racing round behind the after-deck guns, gesticulating and yelling in his anxiety to hasten the reloading; one of the starboard guns for'ard was lying useless on its overturned carriage and dead and wounded men were being carried below. The Frenchman whose bows he had just crossed let fly a ragged broadside, but it was ill aimed and the shot raised a row of white fountains astern. Captain Shovell gave the orders to bring his ship on the larboard tack, heading back towards the French line.

The din of close action was sounding now from van and centre and rear of the French. Through the gaps in the line he could count some eight or nine English ships still holding off with the admiral, so half the fleet had engaged with Châteaurenault's twenty-five on the example of *Defiant* and *Edgar*. But the rest were moving—he could see their masts and sails shrinking into line as they turned their bows towards the enemy. Clow gulped down his emotion. Herbert might yet save the day, and better late than never.

"Braces! Starboard helm—handsomely, now. Larboard broadside, Mr Bream!"

Edgar's slow and ponderous turn was bringing her on the same course as the French and beam-and-beam with a 60-gun vessel three ships astern of the one that had last fired at her. Both broadsides crashed out simultaneously as they drew level. *Edgar* shivered and lurched to the impact of the shot, but though the white splinters flew and there was a chorus of shrieks and groans from the deck she had suffered no damage to spars or rigging, whereas the Frenchman's spritsail-topmast was shot clean away. The English ship had not gathered way enough after her turn to stay level, and her foe drew ahead without further exchange of shot. Captain Shovell transferred his attention to the next astern, separated by a gap of two cable's-lengths from her leader. To his astonishment he saw her turning to starboard to cross his wake, while the canvas of her lower sails came flapping down from the yards to belly out as the breeze filled it, heeling her over until her closed lower gunports were only a foot or two above the waves. Before he could make a guess at the purpose of this manœuvre the double report of *Edgar*'s bow-chasers made him spin on his heel to stare for'ard. Purvis had fired at the Frenchman with the missing spritsail-topmast. She, too, was making away to starboard—and beyond her was the French flagship, already beating back towards the dark line of Crow Head. The whole French fleet, breaking off the action, was putting back into Bantry Bay.

And of course the admiral would not follow them. It would in any case be adding another folly to the worse one of failing to engage closely while he had the chance and the sea-room. There were missing spars and tattered sails to be seen on the retreating French ships, but not one of them had been taken or even badly damaged. They could claim a victory; for he could see the nine English ships who had been with him in the fight now, and there was *Defiant* with only the stump of her mizzen remaining, *Dartmouth* with her foretopmast shot away, and *Mary* with a list that told of shot-holes below the water-line.

The clear note of a trumpet came to Shovell's ear from the flagship, a quarter of a mile distant. Herbert and the other ships were bearing away to the southward and making sail. One by one the truants headed across to join them, while Châteaurenault's fleet sped in good order towards the misty coast of Ireland.

"Messenger!"

"Cap'n, sir!"

Shovell stared at the undersized lad with blackened face who presented himself. "Where's my messenger?"

"I'm him, Cap'n, sir," squeaked the boy. "T'other, he was killed. Cut in half, he was."

"Oh. Then find the first lieutenant and tell him I want him aft here, on the quarter-deck."

But for his own action in following *Defiant* out of the line, that "t'other" would be alive now. There must be many dead beside him; wounded, too. Well, no doubt he would pay his penalty—a court martial, perhaps dismissal. It was small comfort that Edward Herbert would be disgraced, as he deserved. Herbert's shame would be the Navy's.

"Four shot-holes in the bow, sir, larboard side," said Purvis, arriving breathless. "All above water-line, though. First count shows thirteen killed. Parr the bosun's one of 'em—musket-ball in the breast."

Dick Parr of Cockthorpe. Teacher, friend, good servant— and good seaman. Dick would have preferred that last for his epitaph.

"Make all sail, Mr Purvis," said Captain Shovell heavily. "When you've done that, rig a jury spar and hoist the mizzen lateen. We're rejoining the admiral."

III

Spithead danced and sparkled under a brisk breeze and a

bright sun, and the lines of great ships that lay at anchor supported the gaiety of the May afternoon with an abundance of flags and bunting. Captain Clowdisley Shovell, sitting uneasily in the sternsheets of *Elizabeth*'s longboat, saw that his boat was heading for *Defiant*, who lay immediately astern of the flagship. So the admiral had summoned Ashby too; no other captains, or the longboat would have taken a different course on her way from *Edgar*.

Ashby had evidently been ready at the entry port, for he was down the ladder an instant after the boat came alongside. Like Shovell, he was wearing his finest clothes and a fresh-curled wig, and had outdone his fellow captain with a magnificent neckcloth of starched lace.

"H.M. may still be on board," he said, patting the lace self-consciously. "He dined with Herbert, they tell me." His hard square face wore a worried expression. "Know why we're sent for, Shovell?"

"Not I."

Captain Ashby forced a laugh. "I've always wished to be a farmer. If you're anything of a hand with cattle I'll employ——" He checked himself quickly, having realized that the man pulling stroke was in earshot, and pulled a massive watch from his fob. "A minute to go—and we're alongside."

The bowman hooked on to a ringbolt and they went up the ladder to *Elizabeth*'s entry port, Ashby—the senior captain of the two—leading the way. Middleton was at the entry port to receive them, resplendent and portentous.

"You're precise as to time, gentlemen," he said, "and it's as well. His Majesty's in a hurry."

"What's afoot, Middleton?" Ashby demanded anxiously, as they followed him at a quick pace along the alleyways.

"Ssh!" said Middleton over his shoulder, and they came out into the blinding sunlight of the after-deck.

The whole ship's company was drawn up in close-packed

ranks on either hand, leaving clear the space in front of the stern-cabin doors. Captain Shovell had just time to note the resemblance to the preparations for a flogging before the cabin doors opened and the King came out with Admiral Herbert and a stout man in a bright orange coat. Middleton doffed his hat and the two captains did the same.

"Sir, I present Captain John Ashby, *Defiant*, and Captain Clowdisley Shovell, *Edgar*," said Middleton loudly, nudging them forward.

King William glanced sharply from one to the other. His thin, bent figure was dressed all in black, and the famous hooked nose jutted from the shadow of a large black wig. He said something in Dutch to the stout man, who produced from behind him a short dress-sword.

"Kneel!" said Middleton hoarsely from their rear.

They knelt. Clow heard the King's thick foreign tones as from a great distance.

"Rise, Sir John Ashby." There was a light tap on Captain Shovell's shoulder. "Rise, Sir Clow—Sir Clow—you are a knight, sir. Rise."

Shovell got to his feet as if he had just been knocked down and stunned. There was a mist in front of his eyes.

"*Kiss* it!" hissed Middleton urgently.

The King's hand, extended towards him. He bent over the hard thin claw. Someone yelled "Three cheers for the gallant captains, lads," and then Middleton had him by the elbow and was pulling him towards the after companion-way, while *Elizabeth*'s crew cheered their heads off. It was so much like a silly dream that Captain Shovell's mind began to seek at once for rational explanation. If Bantry Bay could be considered a battle, then it was the first battle the Navy had fought for King William; it had been fought against a king who had been Lord High Admiral of the Navy; policy dictated that there should be praise and reward, however undeserved. Presumably it would be called a victory——

"A glass of wine for us all three after that," Middleton was saying.

They were in a neat cabin and the flag-captain was getting a bottle and glasses from a locker.

"His Majesty has ordered every seaman in the fleet to be given a gratuity of ten shillings," he said. "And—this will be news, I think—the admiral is created Baron Herbert of Torbay and Earl of Torrington."

Clow Shovell burst into a roar of laughter. It was so rare a thing with him that the others looked at him in surprise.

"That amuses you, it seems," said Middleton; there was a grin on his face. "We're in confidence here, so I'll confess to finding it amusing myself." He began to fill the glasses. "So would Admiral Narbrough if he were here to learn of it. He had a close knowledge of our noble commander."

"*Had?*"

Captain Middleton looked up quickly at the tone of the question, interrupting his pouring of the wine.

"I am sorry," he said quietly. "I'd forgotten you were an old friend of Sir John. A schooner came in three days ago from St Domingo with the news. Admiral Narbrough died of fever in a Barbados hospital."

FIVE

Clow Shovell woke cold in the darkness and reached for the boat-cloak that hung within reach of his cot in the sleeping-cabin on board *Royal William*. It was not there. Nor (he realized, waking more fully) was he at sea, nor was it perfectly dark. A shaft of moonlight falling between the heavy curtains showed the carved oak pillar of the four-poster bed and cast its shadow across Elizabeth's bare foot protruding from the sheets. His wife. He was Sir Clowdisley Shovell, knight, rear-admiral of the Blue, a year married and twenty-five years away from the ship's boy who had served with Rupert of the Rhine against the Dutch. He was stretched stark naked on the bed, which was why he was cold.

Sir Clowdisley reached down for the blanket, flung to the floor in the violence of their lovemaking. As he pulled it over his nakedness he frowned to feel the size of his paunch; firm enough, none of your soft landsman's flab, but a paunch all the same. At 41, with the softest berth shipboard could provide and even post-captains hastening to do his bidding, a paunch was probably inevitable. He tucked the blanket round his massive body against the chill of early morning—six bells of the middle watch, he guessed it—and since sleep seemed to have deserted him lay with his gaze on the moonbeam to let thoughts and memories have their way.

These past three years had been full of fortune for him. His wooing of Lady Narbrough had been as prosperous as it had been brief, and she had married him immediately on his return from Holland, whither he had convoyed the King;

that task had resulted in his promotion and the realization that William had conceived a liking for him. Perhaps the little Dutchman needed someone to trust in the midst of the intrigues which were once again the fashion in England. So here he was, friend of kings and husband of Elizabeth. It was extraordinary how close they had come, as friends as well as lovers, in that year of marriage, a year in which he had been with her only one month out of the twelve—extraordinary, too, how he felt towards her children by Narbrough as though they were his own. Young John, seven years old now (*Sir* John, because of the baronetcy settled on him in recognition of his dead father's services), besieged him every evening for tales of the Service and always finished by demanding to be ship's boy under his stepfather. John could be taken under his wing as midshipman in seven years' time; young James would have to wait a year longer. Fine lads, both. Well, they might well have a stepbrother before long. He'd done his best to that end. Clow chuckled, remembering.

Elizabeth's gentle breathing was the only sound in the silence of this countryside manor. Different indeed from the ceaseless creak and thud and groan of a night at sea; though two nights from now he would be in his cot hearing those noises (unless Spithead was calm and windless) on board the *Royal William* at anchor. A 100-gun ship. Fortune had been with him in his sea career as well, arranging that he should be on patrol in the Irish Sea with his squadron at the time when Torrington botched that sea-fight with the French off Beachy Head—nine ships of the line lost, and Torrington himself sent to the Tower for his failure. Edward Herbert, Earl of Torrington, at last reaping the reward of his treachery—and of his pretence at seamanship.

No. That was unjust. Clow scowled in the darkness and clenched his fists under the blanket. Torrington, with his ideas about maintaining "a fleet in being", would not have sailed on the foredoomed venture had it not been for Edward

Russell. Jealousy, resentment, intrigue—would the Navy ever win clear of the dirty tangle? He had it in confidence from Burchett the Secretary, who could not be doubted, that Russell had used his influence with the Queen in William's absence abroad, persuading her to order Torrington to attack with his much inferior fleet and hoping (a well-founded hope!) that his rival would be defeated and disgraced. Sir Clowdisley had some acquaintance with Russell, who was his new admiral in command, and he found nothing unlikely in this tale; the only incredible thing was that an officer of the Royal Navy should jeopardize that Navy to further a personal feud. Like Herbert, Russell had offered his services to William long before James Stuart's flight, but it had been Herbert who won the King's favour and the high command and the earldom, and Russell could not forgive him. So Torrington was down and Russell was up. What sort of job would he make of a fleet command? He had been no bad seaman in the days when he captained the *Phoenix*, but since then it appeared that he fancied himself rather as statesman than sailor and perhaps even more as *cavaliere servente*. (It was rumoured that he was strongly attracted to Queen Mary; but Clow was certain that the loyal soul struggling to manage royal matters while her husband was at the wars would have no time for a turncoat like Edward Russell.) Be that as it might, Russell was not the leader the Navy needed at a time like this.

The moonbeam had gone. At his side Elizabeth moved, sighed, and resumed her even breathing. Her husband rested a hand gently on her warm thigh, finding thereby a reassurance which his thoughts could not give him. England was in danger and England had no leaders—except for Dutch William, who had gone to fight the French on the frontiers of his own country. The French had beaten an Anglo-Dutch fleet at Beachy Head and if they fought one more such fight to a conclusive victory it meant the end of English sea-power. Then Louis and his Stuart protégé could invade at their leisure, and as things were at this moment James would find many to support his return to the throne. For William's natural reliance on his trusty Dutchmen in influential posts, combined with a certain arrogance used by those Dutchmen in their dealings with Englishmen, had bred an unrest which Jacobite agents had used with skill to James's advantage. It was a crisis that demanded above all things a signal victory over Louis's new and powerful navy, and that required a skilful fleet commander (Clow was not so modest but he could think of one) which Russell was not. Still, with loyal support even Russell might do better than Torrington——

Sir Clowdisley found himself shifting and sweating under the blanket with the intensity of these anxieties and made an effort to recover his former more cheerful line of thought. Knowlton Court was very well as a home when he was ashore, but it would be John Narbrough's when he came of age and a man should have his own estate. What with prize money and the pay of his rank and sundry other emoluments, he could afford to purchase the Devonshire place he had seen and liked when he had dined with Sir William at Salcombe. Courtlands would suit him and Elizabeth when her sons grew up. By then it was not impossible that he should have risen to be Admiral of the Fleet. Courtlands, indeed, was good enough even for an Admiral of England.

He had reached this lofty point in his reflections when there came a sharp tap at the bedroom window.

Sir Clowdisley threw off the blanket, taking care not to rouse Elizabeth, and went to the curtains. The bedroom was on the first floor and the tap must have been made by a small stone tossed up at the window. Parting the long curtains he peered down at the terrace.

The moon was riding behind dispersed clouds and the terrace was in shadow though the orchard trees beyond lifted silver blossom to the moonlight. A light flashed momentarily by the balustrade of the terrace; a dark lantern. He was about to fling open the window and roar a challenge when he remembered the sleeping Elizabeth. No reason in alarming her. He pushed the casement open gently, feeling the night air cool on his naked body, and muttered sharply, "Who's there?"

The reply came low but clear, a man's voice talking good Norfolk.

"A Cockthorpe man, your honour, along of a message."

"Who sends the message?"

A pause; then, with the hint of a chuckle, "You might say 'tis from him they used to name King James."

"Then damn your eyes and be off." Sir Clowdisley started to close the window. "I want no——"

"Your honour! 'Tis matter o' life and death—life and death for English seamen. And for your ears alone. Draw down, will 'ee, 'tis wholly important."

"Very well." That plea could not be refused. "Go to the end of the stable-yard, at the west side of the house."

"Aye aye, sir."

The three words started a new train of thought in Sir Clowdisley's mind but he had no time to follow it now. Closing the window, he found his breeches and pulled them on. Shoes, the frieze coat with the big pockets, a pistol (unloaded, but that could not be remedied) to go in one of the pockets. Elizabeth was still sleeping soundly. He tiptoed from the room and down through the sleeping house to the back door.

The cobbles of the yard were in shadow as he moved quickly past the rank of outhouses, keeping clear of the stables lest the horses should hear him and make a noise. The man was waiting by the fence that closed the yard, a dark squat figure wearing what seemed to be a round fur hat such as fishermen used.

"Your name, fellow?" demanded Sir Clowdisley as he halted on the inner side of the fence.

"My name's not to the purpose," said the other.

"Perhaps not, since I know it. You're Barnabas Flegg,

deserted from *Edgar* in St Helens three years ago." The pistol came out. "You'll march in front of me to the house——"

"Now hold yow hard, sir," Flegg protested quickly. "There's naught to be got from me that way. I've that to tell as is dangerous as a ton o' gunpowder with a slowmatch burnin' nexter, but my mouth's shut until I hears you swear you'll let me go and forget I've been here. If you've any love for the King's Navy, sir, you'll do that and do it quick," he added, as Sir Clowdisley hesitated.

"Very well. I swear."

"Honour of a gentleman?"

"Honour of a gentleman. But by God, if you've——"

"By'r leave, your honour. I can't be dwindlin' about here so I'll be brief. Mate on a Brixham mule I am now, night-sailing to the French coast. Skipper, he does a trade carrying letters and such—a rum 'un he is, for sure. Often he'll take a squinny at the messages and maybe he makes a trade out o' that too. Anyways, 'twas a week ago we was making a crossing for Cherbourg——"

"What of this message you have for me?"

"I'm puttin' it in a bowline, sir. Me and the skipper, we was quizzing the packets that time——"

One was addressed to a Monseer at Cherbourg. A heated knife lifted the seal and the seal of an inner packet, inside which was a third packet superscribed to *Sa Majesté d'Angleterre*. The letter in it was from Admiral Edward Russell, and signed by him.

"You have this letter?" Sir Clowdisley broke in here.

"No, sir—we was paid to deliver it," returned Barnabas Flegg with dignity. "I'm no thief, and I'm no scholar neither. Skipper, he read it out to me and I've the sense of it in my head. 'Twas an invite to King James to come and rid England of the Dutch——"

Half the army and two-thirds of the Navy would join in the Stuart reconquest, Russell had written; he himself, with

Admiral Carter to second him, would bring over the English ships at the next encounter with the French. His Majesty could rely upon a Catholic rising the moment the news of this coup reached England.

"Which it's my belief," concluded Flegg, "as how that about the Navy's a bloody lie and the rest a lot o' squit. And I'd like to hear that from your lips, sir."

"Of course it's a lie—the Navy's loyal."

Clow's reply came automatically. His thoughts were in turmoil. That Flegg had told the exact truth could not be doubted —the mention of Carter, whose Jacobite sympathies were known to Shovell and very few more, was sufficient proof. And the lie had an uncomfortable basis of truth, too. There was discontent with Dutch arrogance in the Navy as elsewhere in England, and as always the Jacobite plotters were making the most of it. But Russell's message was an enormous exaggeration of the real state of things, born no doubt of his overwhelming passion for self-advancement; a treachery perfectly in character. The man had not a morsel of concern for England or the Navy—was ready to gamble both away on the chance of winning power for Edward Russell and the scaffold for his enemy Edward Herbert.

The sudden barking of a dog in the stables jerked Shovell into realization of the problem that now confronted him, a problem that must be dealt with immediately.

"You did well to come to me, Flegg," he said. "If you'll await me here——"

But Flegg had gone, melting silently into the shadows as soon as the dog barked.

Sir Clowdisley walked slowly back up the yard. The moon was sinking and paling and the east was brightening with the dawn. Post-haste to Portsmouth, where he was to join Russell in two days' time, and confront the admiral with his treachery? Russell would laugh at him. A story told by a deserter—a score of Popish plots with better evidence to substantiate them had been proved non-existent. Go to one of the Ministers with his tale, to Danby or Shrewsbury? The prospect of launching the country into yet another muddy sea of accusation and denial, perjury and intrigue, made him feel physically sick. And there was the shame that must attach to the Navy.

Yet something had to be done, and quickly. The fleet was assembling at Portsmouth with the Dutch fleet to oppose the imminent danger of invasion by the French. At La Hogue in Normandy the great invasion camp held a hundred thousand French and Irish soldiers who waited only for full command of the Channel to be gained by Admiral Anne Hilarion de Coten-tin, Comte de Tourville, before landing to march on London with James Stuart. And at Beachy Head Tourville had proved (at least to his own satisfaction and that of France) that French seamen and ships were far superior to English or Dutch. The test of that must inevitably come within the week.

Clow had paced the yard twice with the dawn wind chilling his close-cropped head before he thought of Elizabeth. His wife was the only person he could trust with Flegg's story; she would believe it because Clow believed it. He would take his problem to her, not merely as a last desperate chance but also because of a faculty he had noted in her of picking the one vital thread out of a tangled matter.

It was with the very faintest of hopes, all the same, that Sir Clowdisley let himself in by the back door and went upstairs to wake his sleeping wife.

II

"I have announced you, sir," said the pompous gentleman in black. "If you will be seated here——"

"It's matter of the greatest urgency," interrupted Sir Clow-disley; a trifle breathlessly, for he had come up two staircases in Kensington Palace at a speed unsuited to his tonnage.

"That", said the gentleman in black with a hint of reproof, "I have told Her Majesty. You need not fear, sir," he added, unbending slightly, "that Her Majesty will keep you waiting. Her Majesty has a most amiable courtesy."

With that, he left the antechamber. Sir Clowdisley, disregarding the invitation to be seated, paced up and down with complete unconsciousness of his quarter-deck roll. With his own coach and a relay of horses bullied out of a Rochester stable he had reached London in three hours from Knowlton Court, having left there at seven after a hasty breakfast of beef and ale. Elizabeth had made him wear the new blue coat with gilt buttons and a pair of breeches he disliked because they looked foppish. "It matters what you wear because the Queen is a woman," she had replied to his protests. Clow would rather have dealt with William, though the King was a foreigner. But Elizabeth had insisted that it was the greatest good fortune that William was absent and that for this matter the royal power was vested solely in the Queen.

"Her Majesty will see you now, sir," said a woman's voice from the inner doorway.

Hat in hand, Sir Clowdisley went rolling in past her without noticing whether she was plain or pretty. A pleasant room hung with paintings; windows overlooking gardens full of tulips in bloom; a lady in a wine-coloured dress seated near the table. He went down on one knee and she rose and gave him her hand to kiss. When he stood up again he saw that she was only half a head shorter than himself. A tall woman, this Mary, and shapely. Not ill-looking by any means, though for his taste fair curls and a more comfortable stature would always take the prize. She had the heavy black brows of her father James Stuart, but the dark eyes beneath them were kind and looked at him straight and honest with none of James's shiftiness.

"They tell me your business is most urgent, Sir Clowdisley," she said. "Use no ceremony, then, but let me hear it, if you please, in plain terms."

Her voice was slow and gentle—not such as he had expected from one who was Queen of England in her own right—and there was a shade of anxiety in her steady gaze that made him suddenly sorry for her. The poor girl (she was at any rate his junior by a dozen years) was wondering if she'd be able to cope with this most urgent business introduced by a rear-admiral of the Royal Navy, without the counsel of her clever Dutchman. It put him so much at his ease that he forgot the introductory speeches he had rehearsed in the coach and plunged straight into his story, which was the tale of that morning's events from the rattle of the stone on the window to Barnabas Flegg's departure; he did not mention the subsequent conference with Elizabeth.

Mary heard him out without interruption, her short-sighted eyes fixed on his face. When he had finished her expression was of sadness and anxiety rather than incredulity.

"You believe this—about the letter written by Admiral Russell?" she asked.

"Your Majesty," said Sir Clowdisley, hasty in his earnestness, "I'd give a fortune to be able to tell your Majesty otherwise, but your Majesty must see that had I not believed it absolutely I'd not have borne such a tale to your Majesty."

A faint smile lightened the Queen's anxious features. "You may address me as 'madam', sir. It is usual." The smile was replaced by a frown. "But why bear the tale to me? Why not to my lords of the Admiralty?"

"I—um—had to shape my course in a hurry, madam. It seemed best to head for the Queen of England."

Mary was not satisfied. "I think you did not shape this course without advice, Sir Clowdisley. It's not what I would expect you to do. Can you assure me that you told no other person of this matter?"

"I—I told my wife, madam," stammered Clow.

The black brows came together. "You told Lady Shovell! Then this ugly business may be bruited about before we can deal with it."

Sir Clowdisley drew himself up to his full six feet.

"I trust my wife, madam, as I trust myself," he said stiffly. "It's everywhere said that your husband does the same."

Mary nodded calmly. "I pardon the impertinence, sir, because I believe it to be true. The King, then, trusts to my wisdom, which impels me to seek the benefit of yours. What do you advise concerning Admiral Russell, Sir Clowdisley?"

The direct appeal took him by surprise although he had his answer ready. As he hesitated, the Queen began to walk up and down; not agitatedly, but with slow and thoughtful steps, speaking as if to herself but loud enough for him to hear.

"This bears out much else that has come to our ears. It's in the blood, perhaps. Russell's father played traitor to Cromwell and his brother was executed eight years ago for treason. Yet I'd not have thought the admiral's ambition would bring him to this. Half the army, he wrote—it could even be true, though the Earl of Marlborough protests its loyalty. But two-thirds of the Navy——" She halted opposite Sir Clowdisley. "Tell me, sir, on your conscience. Are the officers and men of the fleet so ready to side with my father should he invade with the French?"

"I'll tell you how it is, madam." The rear-admiral, a-straddle as if on a tilting deck, emphasized his points by slamming three large fingers of one hand into the leathery palm of the other. "Seamen are ever on the grumble and it's but just to admit they've ever enough to grumble at. But there's not a tarpaulin among 'em that wouldn't fight to stop the French landing, be your father with them or no. Very well. Of the officers, some few are Papists and some few others are jealous of the Dutchmen. Take Richard Carter——"

"We are aware of Admiral Carter's disaffection," Mary said composedly, as he checked himself.

"Well, madam, I'll come to the heart of the matter. Some of us over past years, myself among them, have been at pains to make your Royal Navy a service wherein an order is obeyed without argument or hesitation—captains to admirals, crews

116

to captains. Admiral Russell commands this fleet. If he meets Tourville and orders his ships to join forces with Tourville's, it's odds but half the fleet will carry out the order without stopping to debate."

"But not your squadron, Sir Clowdisley?"

"With the knowledge we share, madam—no. But without it, that's another matter. What do I know of policy? The admiral commands us lesser fry and we take it the King's government directs how he shall command." Sir Clowdisley paused for breath; there was more to be said but his powers of oratory were exhausted. "With Tourville to sail at any moment, Russell can't be replaced. So he must be made to give up his treacherous intention. That's the long and short of it, madam."

The Queen was silent a moment, her eyes looking straight at him but not upon him, as was her short-sighted way.

"I see," she said at last. "And it rests with me to make him give it up. How am I to do that? Shall I summon Admiral Russell to London?"

"With respect, madam, no. And—again with respect—my advice is that you should write a letter to Admiral Russell and send it post-haste to him on board the *Britannia*. It should be in your own hand and signed by you." Clow had repeated these sentences many times during the coach journey to get them by heart, and his voice tended to reveal the fact. "The letter should say that you have heard foul slanders against your Royal Navy, that you refuse utterly to believe them, that you rely on Admiral Russell to exert his known courage and skill in defeating the project for a French invasion. It should add that you trust entirely to the honour and loyalty of the officers and men serving under him."

"But these", said Mary doubtfully, "are arguments Admiral Russell could put for himself. Why should they influence him when I write them myself in a letter?"

Sir Clowdisley picked his words with care. "It has been

rumoured—and I am now in good case to believe it—that Admiral Russell has a—a kindness for your Majesty."

The Queen's pale cheeks reddened and without a word she turned and went to stare out of the window. Clow, fingering his rough chin (there had been no time for a shave) in some apprehension, watched her motionless figure. It was, he supposed, conceivable that William's tall wife might have looked kindly on Russell; he was more of her height than the little hook-nosed Dutchman, and a personable fellow enough if you liked red faces and a dashing manner. More probably, though, she had been flattered by his casting sheep's eyes at her (Russell had undoubtedly done that) and being a woman had cozened herself into thinking him a better man than he was. Would she write the letter? If she did, there still remained the question of whether Russell would be turned by it, as Elizabeth had thought he might. One thing that he knew about Russell, however, made it likely that the proposed treachery was not wholly determined. The admiral hated all foreigners like poison. While it was easily to be believed that he would betray Dutch William on James Stuart's account, it was inconceivable that he should welcome an invasion of Frenchmen. If Russell was now doubting the logicality of his double-dealing, Mary's letter might well turn the scale.

The Queen turned and with a quick firm tread that made the wine-coloured silk rustle loudly passed him and sat down at the table. Her face had regained its even pallor and its composure.

"I shall write exactly as you suggest, Sir Clowdisley," she said. "A courier shall leave London with my letter before noon."

"Your Majesty, I——"

"No more, sir, if you please. We must pray for its success." She held out her hand and he knelt again to take it. "My thanks for this service. You shall have the King's when he returns."

Sir Clowdisley backed towards the door as Elizabeth had instructed him. The lady-in-waiting appeared from nowhere and opened it. Queen Mary, who had already drawn ink and paper towards her, looked round with the quill poised in her hand.

"My thanks also to Lady Shovell," she said with a little smile, "for I think the origin of this letter lies with her."

III

Britannia, 100 guns, flagship of Admiral Russell, was a product of Mr Pepys's building programme of nine years ago. With her length of 146 feet, beam 47 feet, and complement of 780 men she was the largest ship of the Royal Navy, and her great cabin (devoted to the admiral's use) could have accommodated a score of couples for a minuet, musicians and all, if the table and stools and benches had been removed. Only five remained of the thirteen flag officers who had met on board for the Council of War; Russell himself had gone out to see the seven Dutch admirals over the side into their boats. The English vice-admirals and rear-admirals sat together talking in low voices, George Rooke listening patiently to Ashby expounding tactics, Carter discussing uneasily with Ralph Delavall why the admiral had asked them to remain after their Dutch allies had gone. Clowdisley Shovell sat a little apart, silent and imperturbable. The composure of his large bland countenance hid a gnawing anxiety; there had as yet been no word from the admiral concerning the Queen's letter, nor any indication that he had received it.

The Council of War had been notable for the extreme politeness and formality of all present. Not a man there but knew the Dutch ships had saved the English from annihilation at Beachy Head, that Evertsen (who was one of the Council) considered that Torrington had played the coward and left him to bear the brunt of the disastrous fight. So there was cold acquiescence, but no enthusiasm, for the commander-in-chief's proposals for seeking and engaging the French fleet. These were in any case simple, as they had to be. Tourville was known to be ready to sail from Bertheaume Bay, though the strength of his fleet was unknown; the faster ships of the fifth and sixth rates—the "frigates", Russell called them—would sail on the morrow to reconnoitre. The main fleet would sail the following morning, with the thirty-six Dutch ships in the van under Admiral Van Almonde, Russell commanding the centre with Shovell and Delavall to second him, the rear under Rooke with Ashby and Carter. When the frigates reported sighting the enemy it would be the first business of the van to get to windward of the French. As always, the regularity of the line must be maintained in all three divisions.

Sir Clowdisley might have commented on this latter instruction had his thoughts not been occupied with other matters, for he had read Albemarle's treatise on *Dividing the Enemy* and perceived its value. The old plan of engaging in two opposing lines, ship to ship, was stubbornly held to by most naval commanders; but the penetrating of the enemy's line, affording the chance of encircling or doubling on one section of his ships, made more use of seamanship. In especial, a fleet that had not the weather gage and was therefore at grave disadvantage for fighting in line could in this way turn defence into attack. But there must first be a gap by which to penetrate the enemy line.

The admiral came in by the door leading to the half-deck, and the five men fell silent. Without a word Russell stalked to his chair and sat down. His florid face was solemn, and the jutting underlip that gave it always a petulant expression protruded even more than usual. He glanced at his subordinates beneath lowered brows, fidgeted with his wig, touched the lace at his cuffs, and finally began to speak in an embarrassed mumble.

"Requested you to stay—business not concerning the Dutchmen—wish you to understand——"

He came to a stop there. Then, with a suddenness that startled his listeners, he whipped a paper from his breast and raised his voice almost to a shout.

"God damn it all, here's enough of shilly-shally! This letter, gentlemen, is from the Queen's Majesty to myself—but it's for every man in this fleet as well. Attend me, now."

He read the letter out to them, and as he read Sir Clowdisley was able to release the breath he had been holding for a good half-minute. Mary had written precisely as she had promised. Russell read loudly and fast, but he stumbled at the words "I know I can rely on my faithful Admiral of the Fleet" and again at "my trust is placed in the honour and loyalty of the officers and men". When he had finished he placed the letter on the table before him and glared at his five junior admirals.

"Well, gentlemen!" he said in the same loud tone. "Her Majesty places her trust in us. I shall see that it's deserved. If any among us have been disaffected towards the Queen, the rest will know how to deal with them." He laid his hand on the letter. "My secretary has made sixty-three copies of this, one for every ship in the English divisions. My orders are that the captain shall read the letter to his ship's company assembled, and with it a message I have ventured to append, as follows— 'If your officers play you false, overboard with them. Yes, and with me first of all.' That"—he cleared his throat self-consciously—"is signed 'Edward Russell, Admiral of the Fleet.'"

They were staring at him open-mouthed; except Sir Clowdisley, who preserved a strict imperturbability. Inwardly he was marvelling. Russell gave them no time to comment.

"You know the order of sailing," he said curtly, standing up. "Farewell, gentlemen—and God send us Tourville within the week!"

As his boat took him back to the *Royal William* Clow Shovell perceived on reflection that the admiral's action, though unexampled, was not so foolish as it appeared. That signed message with its telling phrases was a most effective way of starting himself with a clean sheet again. But, Lord!—inciting seamen to mutiny if they suspected their officers of Jacobite sympathies! And to think that Clowdisley Shovell the disciplinarian was in some measure responsible for that incitement! Remembering his words to Sir John Berry, off the Gunfleet four years ago, he laughed aloud. Which was so unusual a thing with Rear-Admiral Shovell that stroke pulled short and was very properly reprimanded by the midshipman at the tiller.

So on May 18th the allied fleet weighed and headed down Channel, bearing away southward to make use of the light sou'-westerly. At four next morning they were off Cape Barfleur when flashes and the reports of guns announced the two scouting frigates with news of the enemy. The French fleet was approaching from the south-west, directly up wind from their opponents; and as the morning brightened across a sea of pearl with scarcely a breeze to ruffle the surface the Dutch ships in the van bore up in an attempt to get to windward as they had been ordered. They failed for lack of wind. And now it was seen that the French had only 44 ships to the Anglo-Dutch 99.

Rear-Admiral Shovell, who had stationed himself at the weather rail of *Royal William*'s high poop, rubbed his hands in anticipation of a decisive victory and then hastily clasped them behind his back. It would not do to display emotion before the military. Mustered on the poop at a respectful distance from the admiral were a score of red-coated soldiers, men of the maritime regiment raised last year and named the First Marines. As for Tourville, he had either been misled by the gathering haze and underestimated the force arrayed against him, or was still drunk with the overweening confidence given him at Beachy Head; it mattered little which, so long as he came on. And he was coming on. Let Russell but do his duty (and the weather not play them false) and the French should be taught once for all that La Manche was the English Channel.

The weather was not on the side of the allied fleet that day. The fitful wind died away to light airs, leaving the Dutch ships becalmed in the midst of their effort to get to windward. Tourville was able to bring his van into action without coming near them, and at half-past ten the Red division was replying to the French broadsides at three-quarter musket-shot. Far to the rear, the Blue division under Rooke had been caught by the falling wind and could not come to action. For two and a half hours the great ships of the centre were engaged in an equal struggle, smashing the heavy broadsides at each other whenever they could be manœuvred to close quarters, drifting apart as the inconstant breeze dropped, working their sails to regain position and reopen the cannonade. It was skilful seamanship that brought several of the Dutch ships near enough to join in the fight at last, but by then the threatened fog was drifting towards the Cotentin coast from northward to swallow up the ships and their lesser fog of gunsmoke.

In this fighting Sir Clowdisley had little to do. His flag captain was responsible for fighting and sailing *Royal William*, and the rear-admiral had left the quarter-deck to Captain Jennings and his officers so that he would not be tempted to interfere. But at three o'clock, just before the fog closed down, his chance came. The breeze steadied and strengthened from the north-west, the ship next astern to the Frenchman engaged with *Royal William* had fallen far back, and there was a gap in the French line. Shovell roared his orders. Round to starboard came the *Royal William*, and through that gap with all her division behind her. Starboard again, and they had doubled on the enemy, dividing Tourville's line and bringing the ships of his centre under devastating fire from either hand.

Then came the fog, building its thick white walls between the warring fleets, hiding foe from foe and friend from friend. The gunfire faltered and died away; but in the two hours of this enforced breathing space sudden and prolonged outbursts of firing were heard. Only later did Sir Clowdisley learn how

123

Sandwich groped her way unawares into the midst of the enemy fleet, receiving a murderous fire from all sides and suffering heavy losses including the death of her captain; and how Carter with the Blue division, at last coming up through the fog with the strengthening wind, fell in with the main body of the French and fought a hot engagement for half an hour, his own ship *Duke* bearing the brunt of the fight. He heard with mixed feelings how Carter, once an intending traitor, had died on the quarter-deck with a last order on his lips—"Fight the ship as long as she will swim."

He was able to see with his own eyes how thoroughly Edward Russell had mended his ways. For the fog was blown clear in the early evening, and the disordered fleets were revealed spread to the horizon and all making to the south-ward. *Britannia* was less than a quarter of a mile from *Royal William*, and the scars of her long duel with Tourville's *Soleil Royal* were plain to see—topmasts gone, sails riddled with shot-holes, sides gashed and splintered. And the French flagship—she was discernible through Sir Clowdisley's glass—was flying coastward with the rest of the enemy fleet, in even worse condition.

In the chase that now began Van Almonde's ships managed to come up with the battered Frenchmen and engage for a short time. But nightfall and a renewal of the fog ended the Battle of Barfleur, in which a score of great ships on either side were severely damaged but none taken or sunk. Without the battle, however, there would have been no aftermath. And it was the aftermath, the three succeeding days, that clinched the victory for the allies. The hindmost of Tourville's fleeing vessels were hunted into Cherbourg Bay and the Bay of La Hogue and fifteen of them were totally destroyed. James Stuart himself witnessed the burning of twelve French ships of the line in La Hogue, under the eyes of the Franco-Irish army which was to have invaded England. And the threat of that invasion was banished for a hundred years.

His advancement to rear-admiral of the Red before Barfleur brought Clow Shovell much pleasure; but not so much as the flying splinter that gashed his forearm during the fighting on May 19th. The wound, which he had ignored, turned septic, with the result that on *Royal William*'s return to Portsmouth with the fleet he was conveyed home to Knowlton Court in a high fever. A fortnight of Elizabeth's coddling restored him, and it would be hard to say which derived the more enjoyment from those days, nurse or patient. It may perhaps be conceded that they deserved it.

SIX

The tops'l barge, having brought Shoeburyness on the larboard bow, put her tiller down and headed close-hauled across the ebb current of the Medway towards Sheerness. The rain of a dark September afternoon drummed on the taut canvas of her huge brown sail and brought added discomfort to Sir Clowdisley Shovell, who was squatting on a bale of wet hay in the lee of the hatch with his boat-cloak pulled round him and his hat jammed down over his eyes. Sir Clowdisley endured the discomfort by the simple device of not admitting it. He had chosen, in a huff, to take the first craft that offered down river from Whitehall instead of a coach at the nation's expense; at 45 he was more resolute than ever to maintain the correctness of his decisions, with the corollary that he was more apt to question the correctness of decisions made by the Board of Admiralty. That their lordships were making a foolish decision with these cursed Infernals was what had led him to board a Thames barge and risk a soaking, but he would never admit it even to himself.

Three years of cruising with fleets and detachments, up and down between the Forelands and the Balearics, hounding the French fleet into Toulon and patrolling the Channel, had surely entitled him to the usual shore-leave. All the great ships of the line were now laid up for the winter as was the custom, French and English. It was to be conceded that the successes of the French privateers in the Channel demanded retaliation, but the light squadron needed for the attack on Dunkirk could have been commanded by a commodore instead of by a vice-admiral of the Red. The extensive alterations he had planned for Courtlands, where Elizabeth was now established with their baby daughter and the three step-children, would have to wait. But that was of small moment compared with this further evidence, as he considered it, of muddle and intrigue at the Admiralty and in all the interlinking circles of government. Oh for the strong hand of little Mr Pepys to bring some order to the doings of the Board!

It was a bedlam whichever way you looked at it. Take Russell: disgraced and dismissed after Barfleur for not making a better job of his victory, now First Lord of the Admiralty and said to be next in line for an earldom. Take Lord John Berkeley of Stratton: appointed commander-in-chief in place of Russell, for no other reason, apparently, than his family and influence. There was a tale about another of the Berkeley family, too; young Lord Dursley, barely 16 and pushed up to lieutenant of a 64-gun ship. The silken strings—whether of birth, money, or politics—were again being pulled to make a puppet-theatre of the Navy, and there was no leader of integrity to counter the evil. The King was nowadays wholly concerned with his army, and was still (it was reported) in the shadow of the depression brought on by the death of Queen Mary last year. Even if Pepys were still in office his efforts at reform would be crushed by the powerful Whig Junto of which Russell was one.

" 'Longside the jetty, sir?" hailed the barge's skipper from the helm.

The castellated walls of Sheerness fort and the long dockyard buildings beside it were looming through the rain. Sir Clowdisley got to his feet.

"Aye. Make it touch and go. I'm ready."

Fat Edward Russell—his girth had doubled since Barfleur—wouldn't have been able to face the coming jump. A comforting thought. Clow remembered Russell's bloated face crimson with anger at his scornful criticism of the Infernals. Did the

First Lord know of his visit to the Queen before Barfleur? You could never keep a thing like that from getting about the Court. It would explain why Clowdisley Shovell was very much out of favour just now—and why he had been given this Dunkirk task instead of promotion.

"Here y'are, sir—sharp's the word!"

With miraculous skill the skipper brought his unwieldy craft head-to-wind a foot from the end of the jetty. The jetty planking was four feet above the gunwale, but as the skipper with another warning shout put his tiller over, turning her bows and bringing the wind over the larboard beam, the sudden heel lifted the gunwale at the instant when she began to sheer away. In that instant Sir Clowdisley stepped catlike across the widening gap to the slippery wood of the jetty. The skipper grinned and waved a hand as the barge went flying away on the larboard tack. It was a salute to one man of the sea from another, and put Sir Clowdisley in better humour with himself.

He stalked shoreward along the jetty with the rain and wind lashing the wet cloak about his calves. The east wall of the fort ended close above the foreshore to his right, in front and to the left were the dockyard sheds with a *chevaux de frise* of masts rising from the dry docks behind them. As he noted the sentry in his wooden sentry-box half-way up the path to the sheds he saw half a dozen men issue from the nearest shed and come trotting briskly down past the sentry, headed by a gaunt figure whose breeches and dark coat had a nautical look about them. Perceiving, apparently, that he would reach the inner end of the jetty before them, the gaunt leader halted his men twenty yards up the path, summarily formed them in rank, and was standing stiffly with a hand to his hat as Sir Clowdisley came up. He had a long bony face suggestive of a horse, and his thick black eyebrows were so boldly arched as to give him an expression of perpetual astonishment.

"Very well, sir," said Sir Clowdisley, returning the salute

but frowning in puzzlement. "Who may you be, and what's this?"

"John Benbow, captain, sir," replied the gaunt man in a singularly high and musical voice. "Reception party for vice-admiral."

So this was Benbow, who was to second him in the Dunkirk attack. "A pleasure to make your acquaintance, Captain Benbow. But I was not aware that my visit was expected."

"I had look-outs stationed, sir," said Captain Benbow deprecatingly. "One for the road, one for the river."

"Indeed." Sir Clowdisley was impressed. "Yet it was known only to myself that I proposed to come to Sheerness this afternoon, and that decision I made but two hours ago."

Benbow's equine visage reddened and he showed a certain embarrassment.

"A matter of probabilities, sir," he explained shyly. "It came to my ears that you were summoned to the Admiralty. The chances lay that their lordships wished to instruct you to abridge the delay in sailing for Dunkirk. The delay is occasioned by the construction of these Infernals at Sheerness. Therefore —knowing your reputation, Sir Clowdisley—I judged it very likely that you would come directly from London to Sheerness."

He met the vice-admiral's curious gaze with an innocent stare which had nevertheless a twinkle of amusement in it.

"Well, you were right," said Sir Clowdisley abruptly. "And we're getting damned wet standing here. Lead me to these Infernals."

Benbow snapped a command at the little rank of seamen. They turned as one man and jogtrotted away up the path. The two officers followed at a brisk walk.

"Your fellows go well uphill," commented Sir Clowdisley, holding his hat against the drive of wind and rain.

"They are topmen from *Portland*, my ship, sir," said Benbow. "I see to it that all my hands move about their duties as if at the Double."

The Double was the fo'c's'le name for the rapid drum-beat that summoned all hands to action stations. Sir Clowdisley nodded approval.

"By the by, Captain," he said. "I shall hoist my flag in *Portland* for this expedition. I should have notified you earlier."

He had that moment made this decision. He found Captain Benbow and his methods interesting.

"I'm much honoured, sir," Benbow said equably. "Permit me—we pass through the sheds to the dry dock. We shall find Mr Meesters there." He chuckled uncontrollably as he held the shed door open for Sir Clowdisley to pass. "Your pardon, sir, but the Dutch name in conjunction with the English prefix——"

"Just so," said the vice-admiral drily; mention of the Dutch genius responsible for the Infernals tended to renew his ill humour.

They passed through timber-store and mould-loft, through the all-pervading odour compounded of cut wood and Stockholm tar and paint, towards a sound of hammering; emerging eventually on the platform beside a dry dock wherein was propped the hull of a vessel of some hundred tons or so. Overhead an awning of scantling and boards protected a small army of carpenters from the rain. Up bustled an extraordinary figure—a short and very fat man, round as a ball, dressed in a fur-trimmed purple coat and wearing a wig too small for his large round head. He bowed extravagantly and his wig fell off. He replaced it askew and blinked eagerly at Sir Clowdisley. His little eyes had an odd glitter.

"You are the admiral come to see my Machines," he asserted in a shrill voice.

"To see your Infernals, sir," corrected his visitor.

"Machines, Machines," insisted Willem Meesters, wagging

a stumpy forefinger aloft. "It is more classical." He bowed again, this time holding his wig on with one hand. "So! See then before you, Admiral, Machine Numero Seventeen. Sixteen are done. Tomorrow, seventeen. Tomorrow after eighteen. Tomorrow after, nineteen. Tomorrow——"

"Their lordships have ordered thirty, sir," Benbow put in hurriedly. "It requires only one day to convert a fireship to an —to a Machine."

"I'm well aware they've ordered thirty," retorted Sir Clowdisley. "And what a-God's name they hope to—but enough of that. Mister—um—Mister Meesters"—he caught sight of the twinkle in Benbow's eye and frowned—"I can't wait for the completion of thirteen more Infernals. Today——"

"Machines, Machines, Admiral!" Meesters interrupted, with another wag of his finger.

"Infernals was what I said, sir! Today is the fifth and the ships of your countrymen, which are to accompany the Dunkirk expedition, have been waiting since the second. You say this Infernal will be completed by tomorrow?"

"Most sure he will," crowed Meesters enthusiastically, "and most good will he be! The poor French, to be blown to little pieces! Ah, when you see——"

"Just so. The others, I presume, are at moorings in the Medway."

"Rigged, sir, but not manned," Benbow murmured respectfully. "You could allow four days for rigging this, manning all of them, taking supplies aboard, and having them ready at the Buoy of the Nore."

"Thank you, Captain," said Sir Clowdisley, not without asperity. "I had reached the same conclusion." He turned to the Dutchman. "See to it if you please, sir, that this—um— number seventeen is out and in the hands of the riggers by noon tomorrow. The whole fleet of Infernals will sail from the Nore on the afternoon ebb of September the tenth."

"This shall be done, Admiral." Meesters, hand on wig,

made another bow. "And now I show you him, how he works, eh?"

"Very well, Mr Meesters," said Sir Clowdisley, with a resignation that concealed some curiosity.

Thirty of the things, he reflected as they followed the proud inventor along the edge of the dry dock. If the price paid to the contractor was half what he had heard, someone would make his fortune. More than one person, as like as not. Twenty years ago it would have been nothing remarkable to find half the contractor's fee dropping into the pocket of a gentleman of the Navy Board, and the wind seemed to be blowing from that quarter again today.

"Here now we see all," declared Mr Meesters excitedly, halting a-straddle opposite the midships part of the hull. "Down there in the hold, one hundred barrels of gunpowder —one hundred! Above, a ceiling of planks with liddle holes. Above the ceiling, much combustible—laths, faggots, straw, all a soak and a smear with pitch and resin and tar. So! Above again, here is the deck. And what there?" He flourished his hand. "Cannon-balls of iron and stone, grenades and bombs, iron chains and what-you-will—all these held in a bundle of tarpaulin!"

"Very ingenious, sir," began Sir Clowdisley; but Mr Meesters was not to be deprived of his peroration.

"We ignite with fuse," he declaimed, *crescendo*, "but in the top of the combustible. The flame grow up quick—*whoosh!* The cannon-balls and what-you-will stay quiet, the gunpowder stay quiet. The flame burn up, *whoosh!* Slowly the flame burn down. He burn down, he burn himself through the liddle holes, he drop a spark to the gunpowder—*ker-BLAM!*"

His sudden bellow at the full stretch of his lungs made both Sir Clowdisley and Captain Benbow jump back a pace. Benbow recovered himself in time to grab the fur-trimmed jacket and save Mr Meesters from toppling over into the dock in an ecstasy of illustrative gesture.

"Vastly ingenious, I protest," said Sir Clowdisley hurriedly. "I only hope, sir, that it will prove half as effective as your demonstration. What do you say, Captain?"

"I, Sir Clowdisley?" Benbow said slowly. "I say that nothing so dangerous as Mr Meester's invention has ever before been used by warships."

Mr Meesters beamed with delight, unaware of the drooping left eyelid of Captain Benbow; which Sir Clowdisley, observing, did not entirely approve. It appeared to him that Captain John Benbow was inclined to take serious matters a little too lightly.

"I take my leave, sir," he said curtly. "You will no doubt receive a report on the effectiveness or otherwise of these engines on the completion of the expedition."

"But no need for this, Admiral," protested the Dutchman. "I will myself come with you, to see with mine own eyes."

"I regret," said the vice-admiral coldly, "but that is impossible, Mr Meesters. I bid you farewell."

But Mr Meesters had yet a shot in his locker. He drew a paper from the breast of his fur-trimmed coat and waved it with an apologetic flourish.

"I regret also, Admiral," he said, his round face one large smile. "Here is the Admiral Russell's order. I am to sail upon this expedition, on board the flagship."

II

France, or what Vice-Admiral Shovell could see of it from *Portland*'s quarter-deck, looked a miserable place; a long grey line separating a grey sea from a grey sky. At its nearest point to him the grey line thickened with the roof-tops of Dunkirk and a steeple or two, and he could make out the two long jetties or moles that enclosed the artificial harbour. With his glass he could see a bristle of masts in the harbour—the fleet of privateers who, with their brethren of St Malo, had wrought more damage on English merchant shipping since Tourville's defeat than ever they had wrought before it. There was no getting at those privateers. Between *Portland* and the jetties lay the invisible defences of the port, the Flemish Banks, miles of sandy shallows seamed by tortuous channels which the Dunkirk pilots knew as well as the alleys of their town but which the English had no knowledge of. He had counted on his Dutch pilots for help here, and they had failed him.

Sir Clowdisley turned to glower at the six Dutch vessels grouped half a mile to eastward. Like *Portland* and the other twelve English ships, they were anchored well outside the hidden Banks; they seemed to be huddling sullenly apart, and well they might. Captain Reining of the *Drakesteijn* had stood up for his countrymen as best he could (trust a Dutchman for that), but the fact remained that every Dutch pilot had flatly refused to venture within long gunshot of the Dunkirk forts. Benbow had quietly undertaken to sound the channels with the English boats, and he was about that business now. It was only a matter of minutes before the guns of the fort tried the range and that 20-gun Frenchman anchored outside the east jetty opened fire.

The eight boats were visible as black dots on the wide grey expanse, slowly moving and stopping and moving again as they sought for a two-fathom channel. *Portland* drew sixteen feet (she was only a third of the tonnage of *Royal William*, which drew twenty-three), but she was the largest of his squadron and there were several sixth-rates with a draught of less than ten; the two bomb-vessels drew seven. He shifted his glass to the 20-gun ship and thought he could descry movement on her deck. Benbow had suggested in his usual deprecatory way that the French would have made all possible preparation to meet the precise form of attack he had been instructed to make, and of course he was right. That ship, placed so that her guns and those of the forts could produce a deadly cross-fire, was the proof; doubtless she was protected by a maze of shoals to seaward, for nothing else could explain her confidence in

134

staying there with an enemy fleet of thirty-eight sail—including the Infernals—in the offing. The long delay caused by the manufacture of Willem Meesters's "machines" had given ample time for the Dunkirkers to rig their defences. With the amount of surreptitious traffic there was between Dunkirk and Dover they had probably known every detail of the English plan for the past fortnight.

And there went a gun from the French ship, and another, the orange flashes bright in the darkening afternoon. Sir Clowdisley saw the two tiny white fountains—nowhere near any of his boats—before the reports of the guns came to his ears. He hoped the noise would not bring Meesters on deck; the inventor, who took no other interest in the expedition, had kept his cabin since they sailed from the Nore, desiring merely to be notified when a Machine was to be used. Now the forts were firing, and more flashes came from the ship. He tried to discern the fall of shot again with the glass but the circle of vision was too small and he lowered the instrument, peering anxiously at the black dots that still moved methodically about their task. Forts and ship were firing almost continuously now, and he could occasionally make out the white columns rising and vanishing among the scattered boats. It was useless to tell himself that there was vastly more water than boats for those balls to drop into. A lucky shot could end the lives of a dozen seamen; could end Benbow's life, a far greater loss to the Navy. John Benbow had won the vice-admiral's approval, but he would lose it again mighty quick if he didn't bring those boats out of range and back to the ships.

Sir Clowdisley had the quarter-deck to himself, but he now became aware that he was by no means the only interested spectator. His absorption in the firing had made him deaf to the medley of shouts and cheers and comments from a crowd of hands on the fo'c's'le. It afforded him means of relieving his anxiety.

"Get below there, damn your eyes! Look-outs and watch-on-deck stand firm—I'll flog any other knave who's not below decks in ten seconds!"

His tremendous roar set them jostling like maddened sheep to get to the after-hatch. When he turned to look again shoreward the boats were on their way back and though the firing continued as briskly as ever he could see that every ball was falling short. Two, four, five, seven—eight. All of them safe. Sir Clowdisley was angry with himself for allowing emotion to rise so strongly. If he'd been out there in Benbow's place there would have been none of this worrying and gulping down relief—he would never get used to an admiral's job of sending others into danger. A drizzle of rain blew across, reminding him of Benbow's forecast that bad weather was on its way (damn the fellow, was he never wrong?), but he did not go below for his cloak because *Portland*'s longboat was only half a cable's length away and he considered it courteous to receive Benbow on deck.

The captain, calm and mild as ever, had nothing to say about narrow escapes or being under a hot fire. He had thought it wise, he said, to break off the work of sounding though it had not been satisfactorily completed. If there was a twelve-foot channel to the harbour, as there must be, the boats had not found it. On the other hand, there should be enough water for the bomb vessels and the Infernals.

"The only other ship that would get close inshore tomorrow, sir," he added, "is the *Charles*."

For a moment Sir Clowdisley saw again the blue Mediterranean, and Matt Aylmer laughing and waving on *Charles*'s tiny quarter-deck. Matt was a vice-admiral like himself now, and doubtless at his ease with a flagon ashore.

"*Charles* mounts thirty 6-pounders," he said. "Popguns, but I'll wager they'd do more damage than Meesters' damned Infernals."

"Yes, sir," said Benbow. "And the mortars more than either. If I may venture to suggest it, you could send in

Charles and the bombs in the morning. It's nigh on neaps and if they weighed an hour this side of high water they'd have two hours for bombardment before returning." He turned his mild brown eyes on the vice-admiral. "The pity is, sir, that the mortars are bound to hit houses in the town while they're ranging on the shipping."

"I can't help that," returned Sir Clowdisley brusquely. "We have to teach these rogues of Dunkirk privateers that we can hit them even if we can't catch them. That's the will of their lordships. It's also their will that I use these Infernals. Pray venture to suggest something on their account, Captain."

"Certainly, sir. If the wind's fair, you could try some of the Infernals in the afternoon. There'll be enough water for them. Cole and Robinson are the two likeliest commanders. Cole has——"

"The *Abram's Offering*. I know my men, thank you, Captain. And Robinson has the *William and Mary*. I'm informed—I find it hard to credit—that they have volunteer crews."

Benbow smiled faintly. "It's true enough, sir. I think it must be the novelty. And *William and Mary* has a noble volunteer to suit her name—Lord Dursley, grandson of the Earl of Bedford. He holds a lieutenant's commission and he's second to Robinson."

"Indeed." Sir Clowdisley felt the rain soaking through the shoulders of his coat. "Well, I'll use those two craft if the wind serves. I shall go below now. Call me if the Dunkirkers make any move. I believe you've had no sleep since we left the Nore?"

"No, sir."

"Then I recommend you to turn in, as I shall do. And, Captain Benbow—do not, on any account, rouse that—that infernal Dutchman."

"No, sir," said Benbow solemnly.

But it appeared that the excitability of Willem Meesters found its compensation in an inordinate capacity for sleep, for

137

he was not disturbed by the considerable activity on *Portland*'s decks in the small hours of next morning. The threatened change in wind direction and force was heralded by a driving squall that set the ships snubbing and snatching at their cables and necessitated a second anchor for *Portland*, with the shouting and banging attendant upon getting it out. With the coming of grey daylight the squall died away, leaving a strong and steady westerly blowing under low dark skies. It was a fair wind for the attacking force, and the flagship's boat had taken Sir Clowdisley's orders to *Charles* and to the bomb-ketches *Salamander* and *Firedrake* before he had finished his breakfast of beef and bread and wine. An hour later he was on the quarter-deck with Benbow, watching the three small ships heading away towards Dunkirk with a beam wind.

Charles, giving the anchored French ship a wide berth, edged in towards the west mole, the fort guns opening fire as soon as she came within range. She would be keeping the lead going continuously as she began to sail up and down with her guns blazing at full elevation, trying to drop the shot beyond the mole. Sir Clowdisley tried to discern the fall of shot with his glass, but the blurred grey surface of the sea was flecked with whitecaps and he could make out nothing to the purpose. A risky business for *Charles*, this. She had orders to maintain speed, and a moving target would make things difficult for the French gunners; but they had solid unmoving ground under their 32-pounders, which doubled the chance of hitting. He resolved to hoist the blue flag which was *Charles*'s recall signal in twenty minutes' time, and shifted his attention to the bomb-ketches.

The squat, beamy little ships had brought-to much nearer to their squadron, possibly (thought Sir Clowdisley) within long gunshots of the forts but beyond the range of the French ship. They looked very odd with their massive mainmasts and no foremasts—the fore-decks were occupied by the enormous mortars, capable of hurling balls or stones up to two hundred pounds' weight. *Salamander* and *Firedrake* would fire missiles of less than half that weight in order to obtain the maximum range. They would be using their springs now—he could see them turning, each on its axis, as the second cable passed from stern to anchor was hauled upon. And there went the first shot. The detonation of the charge was loud even at that distance and in spite of the wind. Both bomb-ketches began to fire at regular but long intervals; it was impossible to see where their missiles went.

"My Machines!" screeched Mr Meesters, popping up beside him. "You use my Machines and not tell me!"

He was without his wig and the wind blew his fur-trimmed coat about fat bare legs. Sir Clowdisley turned to glower down at him.

"I do not use your Mach—Infernals, sir," he retorted, "until this afternoon. Pray return to your cabin."

"I make insistence, Admiral," said Mr Meesters, making vain endeavours to close the front of his coat, "for instantly informing when my——"

"You'll take an ague, sir," interrupted Sir Clowdisley. "Go below this moment. Captain Benbow does not permit nakedness on his quarter-deck."

Mr Meesters, spluttering and clutching at his inadequate garment, retired. Sir Clowdisley caught Benbow's eye and hastily erased the grin from his own features.

"Hoist the recall for *Charles*, Captain, if you please," he ordered.

Charles, when she came near enough to be examined, showed shot-holes in main and foresails but seemed to have suffered no hits on her hull. Sir Clowdisley continued to watch the leisurely firing of the bomb-ketches, on which the forts were now firing at extreme range and without apparent effect. When at length he gave orders for their yellow recall-flag to be hoisted and they came plunging and bucketing back over the grey-white chop they, too, showed no sign of being hit.

Their reports were brought to him as he took his solitary dinner (broiled mutton, tolerably well done by *Portland*'s cook) and told little beyond the fact that their shots had cleared the moles and fallen either in the harbour or in the town beyond.

A petty business, he reflected, sipping at a glass of Canary. Waste of a vice-admiral's services—waste of a first-rate captain like Benbow. How old was Benbow? Well over forty, and still a captain. No money, no influence—no birth. And here was this grandson of the Earl of Bedford, Lord Dursley, a lieutenant at 16 and like to be a captain before he was 20. Still, Dursley was no lily-liver, to volunteer for an Infernal; he was young enough to have undertaken the venture as a bravado, but the fact remained that it was a mighty perilous venture. These Infernals had to be sailed until they were so close to their targets that there was no possibility of failure (which meant very close indeed) and then the fuse had to be lit and the ship abandoned, almost certainly under a murderous fire from the enemy. That was if all went well. There were plenty of chances of mishap before the fuse was lit, with all that explosive stuff aboard, not to mention the rottenness of the ships—for only condemned vessels had been used—and the amount of drilling and boring they had undergone at Meesters's orders. It was to be expected that Meesters would go into a frenzy at the sight of his beloved Machines actually in use; perhaps a couple of Benbow's men ought to be stationed ready to grip him if he offered to prance overboard.

When the time came, however, Willem Meesters displayed no excitement, nor even enthusiasm. Holding apart from Sir Clowdisley and *Portland*'s officers, who were gathered at the quarter-deck rail to witness the attempt, the little man—his rosiness changed to a yellowish green—clung to the belaying-pin rack at the foot of the mizzen and watched with lack-lustre gaze the departure of *Abram's Offering* and *William and Mary* across the choppy seas towards Dunkirk. The ebb countering the wind had wrested the flagship broadside-on to the waves, and her jerky rolling motion was proving too much for the inventor's stomach.

Away raced the Infernals, with the wind just abaft the beam. In that whipped-up sea, Sir Clowdisley reflected, the boats would have no easy time winning back to the squadron, though the tide would be with them. *Abram's Offering* began to diverge to southward from her consort's course; her object was to get dead to windward of the harbour entrance before lighting and abandoning, in the hope that the explosion would take place among the shipping inside. *William and Mary* was to bring up alongside the east mole; Meesters (before he had reached his present state) had been confident that an explosion could destroy a considerable length of the mole.

Both forts and the anchored ship began to fire as soon as the Infernals came within range. In the dull dark afternoon light the orange flashes, mere sparks in the distance, were the only points of colour in a blue-grey monochrome. But the atmosphere was clear now, there being no rain, and with his telescope steadied on the shoulder of Benbow's second lieutenant Sir Clowdisley could follow the course of the two little vessels.

There went *Abram's Offering*, straight towards the guns of the western fort—they must be firing at a thousand yards now. She should be to windward of the entrance. Yes, she was turning. And her topmast was gone, shot away. But her courses were carrying her on, and it looked as though Cole had headed her accurately to pass between the moles. The two boats appeared suddenly astern of her, and he let out his relief in a string of oaths muttered under his breath. Hardly had he done so when *Abram's Offering* disappeared in a brilliant glare, a volcano of flame that sank and then sprouted in a ruddier tongue of fire. She was still a good quarter of a mile outside the harbour entrance.

Sir Clowdisley's roar cut short the babel of exclamation and comment. He swung round upon Meesters.

"Thirty seconds!" he snapped. "You told me it was a five-minute slow-match!"

The inventor's reply came feebly and after some convulsive gulping. "The match, Admiral, he is five minutes. But a liddle spark——"

"Damn and blast your liddle sparks!" Sir Clowdisley steadied his telescope again. "I see the boats—both afloat, and thank God for it. If there's a man left unhurt in them, it's more than we deserve."

"*William and Mary* is at the mole, Sir Clowdisley," said Benbow. "I can see both her boats putting off, and under a hot fire from the Frenchman."

The vice-admiral swung his glass slowly and picked up the vessel rocking against the mole, and then the pair of boats pulling away from her. The sparkle of bright flame from the French ship, half a mile from them, showed that she was firing her guns as fast as they could be loaded and laid. Five minutes —less, now—before the Infernal blew up. And the boats were coming very slowly back, against the wind. They'd hardly be out of range before the explosion came. What of the others? There they were, almost half-way back already; enough sound men left, then, to pull so lustily. As for their Infernal, she was just a smouldering mass low on the water, drifting harmlessly on the ebb.

"*William and Mary*'s boats have stopped, sir," said Benbow. "Seven minutes gone since they abandoned. I fancy——" He checked himself. "Yes, by—yes, sir. One of the boats is pulling back to the ship."

Sir Clowdisley opened his mouth and shut it again. Swearing was no use. He devoted himself in silence to the dim and shaky circle of the lens, wherein the boat could be seen making that perilous return journey—through the storm of enemy shot to a hundred barrels of gunpowder that might explode and let loose a deadly hail at any moment.

Suddenly the enemy's cannonade stopped. Someone had at

last realized that this was another explosive ship and could be detonated by a French ball as well as by an English fuse. The boat's black speck vanished from Sir Clowdisley's purview as it merged with the hull of the Infernal; and the silence across the water seemed to have induced a tenser silence on *Portland*'s quarter-deck. There was a gasp of released breath when the boat reappeared pulling hard away from the Infernal, but no one spoke except Benbow, who had his watch in his hand.

"One minute gone. Two minutes. Three minutes. Four _____"

Up spurted the tongue of flame, licking her masts and catching the sails, and now the watchers gave a lusty cheer—which Sir Clowdisley, though he did not join it, forbore to repress. And hard on the heels of the cheering came a blinding flash and thunderous detonation. The second Infernal had blown up little more than a minute after she had been set on fire. So much for Meesters's "liddle holes".

"Hold still!" he growled at the second lieutenant, and sought with his telescope for the boats.

One was still afloat. So was the other. They had made more distance away from the danger area than had Coles's boats before the explosion; all the same, it looked as if these Infernals delivered their eruptions vertically upwards. He turned his glass on what was left of *William and Mary*. The explosion had left no flame, only a line of smouldering fragments along the base of the mole. And the mole itself showed still the same uninterrupted outline. There was no breach—no damage at all, so far as he could see.

Sir Clowdisley snapped his telescope shut and thrust it into his pocket.

"Captain Benbow!" he said abruptly. "Summon Captain Robinson's boat when it comes within hailing distance. I wish to commend the man who returned on board to relight that fuse."

"It would certainly be Captain Robinson himself, Sir

Clowdisley," said Benbow. "I know him, and he'd allow no man but himself to do it."

"Then it's Captain Robinson I wish to see. And now——"

Sir Clowdisley swung round, took two paces, and grasped Mr Willem Meesters by the shoulders, none too gently.

"I trust you're satisfied with your damned, blasted, infernal Machines?" he said between his teeth. "I've risked two good captains and crews to no purpose—d'ye know that?"

Mr Meesters, who was limp as a puppet in his grip, made no reply. Sir Clowdisley perceived the reason for this in the nick of time. Twisting the little man round, he bore him to the quarter-deck rail and bent him over with his pallid face to the grey-green waves below.

"Feed the fishes, man," he adjured him. "It's all you're good for. And if I thought there was a shark among 'em, by God I'd give him something bigger to swallow!"

III

The squally afternoon had darkened to a premature twilight by the time *William and Mary*'s boat came alongside the flagship. In *Portland*'s stern cabin the lantern hanging from the deck beams swung with the uneasy roll of the ship, casting a fitful light on the slim figure that stepped from the shadows at the cabin door to stand before the vice-admiral at his table. Sir Clowdisley stared. This was not Captain Robinson. A face of rare beauty—masculine, but beautiful as Apollo; the face of a boy, smooth and unblemished, yet with the pride and confidence of a man. Wide grey eyes met his scrutiny, finely pencilled brows lowered with a hint of resentment as it was prolonged.

"And pray who are you, sir?" he demanded, brusquely because he was startled and strangely moved.

The boy threw back his head, haughtily and with unconscious grace. He was coatless, in breeches and shirt, and his head (he wore no wig) was covered with small clustering curls that glinted gold in the lamplight. The shirt was blackened and a torn ruffle hung from its open front, which revealed a throat white and perfectly modelled.

"I am James, Lord Dursley," he returned; and added, rather as an afterthought, "sir."

So this was the young upstart who was being pushed up through naval rank by the Whig aristocracy. Sir Clowdisley found himself unable to feel the animosity he should have felt.

"Your pardon if I spoke discourteously," he said. "I had expected Captain Robinson."

"Captain Robinson will be *hors de combat* for a day or two," replied the boy negligently. "The French contrived to take a slice from our mainyard on the way to the mole and dispatch it against Robinson's skull—a rare thwack, I protest. But I apprehend it's not serious."

"Then it was not Captain Robinson who returned to relight the fuse?"

"Without doubt he would have done so. The man is a very tarpaulin but he has courage. No, Sir Clowdisley—it was I who went on board."

Dursley's manner, palpably unsuited to a junior lieutenant addressing a vice-admiral, should have earned him a reprimand. Sir Clowdisley had no thought of giving one. He stood up, went round the table and grasped Dursley's hand.

"It was a bold deed, sir, and boldly done," he said. "You have earned my esteem and commendation."

"Thank you, Sir Clowdisley. I but did my duty."

There was a faint smile on the youth's lips—a trifle too red and full for perfection—as he withdrew his hand from the older man's retaining clasp.

"I trust, however," he added, "that your commendation will reach the ears of their lordships at the Admiralty. I'll not conceal from you, Sir Clowdisley, that I'm ambitious of advancement."

Sir Clowdisley, with a warmth unusual in him, gave an

assurance that their lordships should hear of it in the strongest terms; and (for he found it difficult to let Dursley depart) requested an account of the relighting of the fuse on board *William and Mary*. The boy waved a hand in graceful deprecation; and the lamplight struck green fire from a large emerald in the ring on his middle finger.

"Why, the knaves murmured at pulling back again," he said carelessly. "Anxious for their lousy skins, no doubt. But Robinson was lying senseless and I had the command."

So back they had gone, and Dursley, boarding the Infernal alone, had found the slow-match extinguished after burning only one-third of its length; an accumulation of salt water in which it had been lying had soaked through the canvas tube and dampened the powder core. With his knife he had frayed open the dry continuation of the match, and flint and steel had ignited the powder train once more. After which——

"You may wager I made myself scarce *velis et remis*," said Dursley with a boyish grin, "for I'm none so bold but I prefer my body in one single piece." He glanced down at his clothes. "I regret, Sir Clowdisley, that I could not appear in more polite attire than this, but an Infernal is no place for a gentleman in the garb of his rank."

"It's no place for a seaman, gentle or simple," nodded Sir Clowdisley with feeling, "and their lordships shall know my opinion."

With that, Lord Dursley took his leave and the vice-admiral turned to his business of reports and orders, which was considerable. He felt himself oddly disturbed by Dursley's visit, without knowing why; and for some minutes was unable to concentrate on the dispositions of his squadron for the future. Was it, he wondered, that this James was just such a youth as he would have wished his own son to be, had he begotten one? Perhaps that explained his feeling for the boy, the strong attraction he had experienced in his presence. The hint of callousness and arrogance in his manner (Sir Clowdisley was forced to admit this) was but natural to his youthfulness and noble birth, easily to be excused in one in whom so many human graces were displayed. The commendation he had asked for should be dealt with the first of all his business. Sir Clowdisley picked up his quill and drew a sheet of letter-paper towards him. He had quite forgotten his hatred of aristocratic sprigs who were made lieutenant at 16 through influence and political jobbery.

He addressed his report to the Admiral In Command, as he was bound to do. Of Mr Meesters's Machines, when he came to that subject, he wrote a downright condemnation, adding that he suspected they were "an Invention to swell the projectors' accounts". He was sending the remaining Infernals and small craft into the Thames forthwith, he told Lord Berkeley of Stratton, since the weather was worsening and gales were to be expected; but he purposed to betake himself off Calais with the larger vessels and bombard that place, thereby giving the French a lesson which Mr Meesters and his Invention had failed to teach them.

The matter of John Benbow required a separate document, Under the system in force, the main essential for obtaining promotion from captain to rear-admiral was a full recommendation by a flag officer of vice-admiral's rank or above. Sir Clowdisley penned a strong one. His credit with their lordships would have to be unconscionably low, he told himself, before they ignored that. And now the orders for the squadron. It was later when he turned in, and later still when recurrent images of young James's handsome face—the turn of his head, the easy grace of his body—departed and allowed him to sleep.

On September 17th Sir Clowdisley led a reduced squadron of six English warships and six Dutch through the storm-tossed waters off Gris Nez to subject Calais to a gruelling bombardment which no port could have expected in such weather. The citadel and fort on the dune-island took the full force of *Portland*'s broadside at half a cable's-length and suffered accordingly. A number of privateer schooners beyond the harbour wall were damaged and a number of buildings hit. It was a satisfactory demonstration that the guns even of fourth- and fifth-rates could hurt the enemy when no gimcrack Infernal could get near him. It was also a remarkable feat of seamanship, for which Sir Clowdisley was reponsible. But his satisfaction was offset by perturbation of spirit. He perceived, though dimly, that his affection for James, Lord Dursley, was not that of a father for his son.

SEVEN

Little Mr Pepys was dead. The turn of the century had brought no manifest blossoming of the Royal Navy into a great sea power, such as he had dreamed of; only in the increasing efficiency of the Navy Office, the steady tightening of ship discipline conjointly with improvement in conditions and pay, the novel discovery of politicians that the Navy was no longer to be a pawn in their intrigues, was his strong and continuing influence discernible. One or two in high places—among them Sir Clowdisley Shovell, admiral of the White—cherished the vision and worked for a Navy that should command the seas. They saw, though with imperfect clarity, that such command could be the deciding factor in the great war now raging across Europe; a war ostensibly to resolve whether a French or an Austrian candidate should occupy the vacant throne of Spain, but fundamentally the test of England's ability to oppose the spreading aggression of France. But the masters of these far-sighted few had not the same vision.

William was dead. Anne, daughter of James Stuart, was on the throne and Jacobite plots at an end for the time being. Before his death William had shown his awareness of one aspect of the Navy's potential by sending Vice-Admiral John Benbow with a squadron to the West Indies to break the French sea-power there, but to the end the King held that ships in the Channel or the Mediterranean could bear little part in a war which must be won on the battlefields of Europe. And Marlborough, the new warlord of England, who could (as he secretly boasted) "turn the Queen about his little finger, were she not so fat", saw the Navy only as a means of creating diversion by feint attacks on enemy coasts. In vain Shovell and Rooke and others prayed for a fleet base in the Mediterranean, such as Tangier had been in Charles's time, which would enable English warships to bring to a final reckoning the enemy fleets that harboured there. They were employed in petty raids or blockades of individual ports that failed because of their intermittence. "Piddling piracies," Sir Clowdisley declared them, with a stern eye to see that his two stepsons nodded dutiful agreement.

This was in the course of a winter evening's discussion by the fire at Courtlands. Elizabeth was not present, having learned by long experience that nothing would be talked of but Navy matters when her husband took wine with John and James Narbrough. Both the young men were commissioned lieutenants; Sir John, uncannily resembling the Sir John Narbrough who had been young Clow's hero at the Four Days' Battle, was 22 and his brother 21.

"We're hamstrung without a Mediterranean base," said James, who knew well what his stepfather liked to hear. "The government should lease Tangier from the Moors, sir—then the French would no longer be safe in Toulon."

John Narbrough, more thoughtful and serious than James, spoke deliberately and after a pause. "Why lease a naval base? Why not take one?"

Sir Clowdisley bent disapproving brows. "Carry Tangier by assault? War with Morocco?"

"Not so, sir. We're already at war with Spain, since the Dons support this Philip of Anjou who is King Louis's protégé, so it's a blow in the fight if we seize a Spanish port. It was Gibraltar I had in mind."

"Gibraltar!" Sir Clowdisley was inclined to be scornful. "Poor harbourage, surely. I was there with *Nonsuch* in '81 and nigh sunk at anchor with a sou'-westerly blowing."

"Yet", said John resolutely, "the anchorage could hold a

fleet, and it's exposed only to the south-west. Consider also, sir, that Gibraltar's inside the Mediterranean, five leagues east of the Strait, while Tangier's outside on the African coast. And there's place for a dockyard on the west—I've been there, you'll recall, in *Swiftsure* three years ago."

"Gibraltar's a very strong fortress," objected James. "The Spaniards have forts and batteries there and they'll have a big garrison well prepared now that the war's——"

"You speak in ignorance of Spaniards, lad," interrupted his stepfather. "Spaniards are never well prepared. They had a strong fleet once and what is it now but rotten timber? It's odds but the Gibraltar defences are in like case. I wonder——"

The entrance of his wife with their nine-year-old daughter, to bid him good night, broke up the discussion and it was not renewed. But the matter of it stayed in Sir Clowdisley's mind; and it was there six months later when he sailed with a squadron of fourteen Dutch and English ships of the line to reinforce Admiral Sir George Rooke at a rendezvous off Tangier.

The idea behind this movement of warships was characteristic of the Queen's General. Marlborough, with Europe for his board, was manœuvring for the final checkmate at Blenheim and mustering every strategy he could think of to ensure success. The best use he could imagine for the Navy was, as usual, a feint attack—a big demonstration off Toulon to worry the French with fears of troop landings in the south. Rooke and Shovell with fifty-one ships could effect this, and if the inferior French fleet at Toulon came out to be destroyed, so much the better.

So on July 16th of that year, 1704, the two fleets met at the rendezvous and sailed slowly eastward as a single unit, Sir Clowdisley by Sir George's invitation leaving the 96-gun *Barfleur*, in which his flag was hoisted, to join Rooke on his flagship *Royal Katharine*. They had passed the Straits, but were less than a league east of Tetuan, when a fast galley out of Lisbon overtook them with dispatches. Within an hour the fleet had been ordered to heave-to and a council of admirals and senior captains summoned for the hour of sunset. Some thirty minutes before the members of the council were due to arrive, the two admirals were taking the air together on *Royal Katharine*'s quarter-deck, pacing and turning side-by-side with hands clasped behind backs and bewigged heads nodding in confidential talk. Around them the host of great ships sat almost motionless on a sea of shot-silk, whose darkening blue was veined with orange-red from the huge ball of the sun suspended in the haze above the purple hills of Rîf.

Some time after the battle of four weeks later, a London wit dubbed the brother admirals "the Great Twin Brethren"; and indeed they were not unlike in more ways than one. George Rooke had not Shovell's height, but he could match him for weight, and his broad face had the same obstinate chin and stubborn set of the lips. But whereas Shovell's eyes were small and keen ("a quiet-mannered, comely gentleman with oddly bright eyes," a friend wrote of him) Rooke's large brown eyes were always shadowed with depth of thought. He was involved in politics, a dedicated Tory; which was the one aspect of Rooke of which Sir Clowdisley—himself Member of Parliament for Rochester, but a most inactive Member—disapproved, holding that the Royal Navy had nothing to do with faction. By virtue of his commission Sir George was commander-in-chief of this expedition, and he was also just senior in rank to his fellow admiral, but Clow liked him, admired him as a seaman, and would have been content to serve under him in any circumstances.

"If I could but ignore the damned dispatches!" Rooke was saying with an unusual show of irritation. "Consider, sir—the Count of Toulouse has won through from Brest to Toulon while our backs were turned, which means the bulk of the French naval strength, fifty ships and more, in Toulon. And here are we ready to deal the blow that will crush them. Now comes this royal command to put about and bombard Cadiz instead."

" 'An attempt on Cadiz' were the precise words, I fancy." Sir Clowdisley brought a hand from behind his back to rub his chin reflectively. "If that means we're to attempt to capture the place, it's plainly impossible without an army. And your royal command came not, sir, from Her Majesty of England."

Rooke jerked his shoulders impatiently as they turned together at the poop ladder and began the return walk.

"It came through our minister at Lisbon from King Charles of Spain—he calls himself that already—and the King of Portugal. The consequences of disobedience would be much the same."

"By your leave, Sir George, any court martial would acquit. The insufficiency of our land force can't be denied."

"They might say these eighteen hundred fellows of the Marine regiment were sufficient."

"For an assault on a place other than Cadiz," said Sir Clowdisley, "they might be sufficient."

"What other place?" demanded Rooke suspiciously.

Sir Clowdisley hesitated. Rooke was just as obstinate as himself, would receive his suggestion (it had flashed into his mind only a minute ago) with just the same refusal to entertain it he himself had at first opposed to John Narbrough. A bait was needed—and by God he had it!

"Can you truly conceive, Sir George," he said, "that Toulouse will bring his ships out of Toulon to meet us? With nothing to gain and all to lose?"

Rooke's frown at the first question was replaced by a smile at the comical euphony of the final words of the second.

"We'll make a wit of you yet, friend Clowdisley," he said, his mood changing for the better. "But in seriousness, sir, you have put a finger on my own blackest doubt. Toulouse is no fool. He may well elect to stay in harbour."

"I know how we can fetch him out, and for certain."

"Then tell me!" cried Rooke eagerly. "If you can convince me I'm for ever your debtor."

"Take Gibraltar," said Sir Clowdisley.

Sir George halted abruptly and they faced each other, Rooke's expression changing rapidly from incredulity through speculation to excited acceptance.

"By all the saints!" he exclaimed. "We can try it—and if we succeed the French fleet will have to come out. With Gibraltar an English fortress they'd never leave the Mediterranean again." He began to walk swiftly along the deck with Sir Clowdisley half a pace behind. "And suppose we could hold Gibraltar. Make it our base as Tangier was. Build dockyards, stores—why, man, Cadiz is a fiddlestick to this!"

He stopped as Fletcher, his flag-captain, approached and swept off his hat.

"Your pardon, Sir George—*Kent*'s boat coming alongside, Rear-Admiral Dilke in her. And other boats approaching."

Rooke's unwonted excitement was instantly mastered. He turned to Shovell.

"We must to the great cabin, Sir Clowdisley. I fancy we shall carry the council with us to a man in the matter we've just discussed."

Remembering his own initial doubts, Sir Clowdisley was not so sure. And within half an hour he was hearing his uncertainty justified.

The council of six admirals and twenty-five senior captains, with Prince George of Hesse who commanded the Marines, crowded *Royal Katharine*'s stern cabin. Clow found himself looking eagerly for the captain of the *Boyne* though he knew very well he was not summoned; James, Lord Dursley, a postcaptain at 24, had not the required seniority. The assembly heard Rooke's calm explanation of his orders and were unanimous in approval of his decision against attacking Cadiz. His announcement of the alternative objective, however, provoked surprise and some consternation, which resolved itself into an opposition of some half-dozen headed by Rear-Admiral Byng. George Byng, who had come out with Shovell as his second, was a level-headed seaman of 40, whose undoubted courage was tempered with stubborn prudence. His objection was a plain statement of fact.

"Gibraltar", said he bluntly, "has been considered impregnable for the past two centuries, by every nation whether of east or west."

"Including the Spaniards," Rooke said quickly, and looked round the assembled officers. "I fancy we all know the Dons, gentlemen. They'll trust to that reputation, two centuries old as Admiral Byng tells us, and let it suffice for the protection of Gibraltar. What's the odds they haven't improved their defences since Charles the Fifth's time?"

"A hundred to one," suggested Captain Crow of the *Shrewsbury*.

"Two to one, at the least," amended Rear-Admiral Sir John Leake cautiously.

"We'll vote on this, then," said Rooke; he glanced towards the Dutch officers. "Vice-Admiral van Wassenaer, have your countrymen understood the question?"

"Perfectly, Sir George," answered Van Wassenaer, nodding and beaming. "Understood also is how the French must come out and fight us if we capture this place."

That brought a buzz of comment from those who had not perceived the corollary. When the vote was taken, on show of hands, only Byng and two others were against the project.

"This fleet, then, will attack Gibraltar as soon as our dispositions are made." The Admiral smiled pleasantly at Byng. "Do you wish to remark further on the matter, sir?"

"I still think the risk of failure is too great," Byng said steadily. "But I'm well content to take it in this present company." He hesitated, then added with a touch of defiance: "My concern is only lest we should weaken ourselves before we engage with the French fleet."

"No one here would imagine that George Byng's concern was for anything else," returned Rooke equably. "Very well. The attacking force must clearly be a detachment from the fleet —say twenty sail of the line—with a rear-admiral in command. I appoint Rear-Admiral George Byng to command the assault."

Byng flushed with pleasure. "Thank you, Sir George," he said. "I count it an honour."

Perhaps Admiral Shovell had entertained some slight hope of the appointment; but it was not for a full admiral to command a squadron, and the inshore waters of Gibraltar Bay did not afford sea-room for the manœuvring of a fleet. He had to content himself with a distant view of the operations (whose momentous nature he dimly perceived, though not with Rooke's comprehension of their possibilities) from the anchorage of the main fleet, in the Bight of the Bay off the Guadaranque river.

The taking of Gibraltar occupied three days. First the bombarding squadron of twenty-one Dutch and English ships took position opposite the town and forts, which opened a sparse fire upon them, though without doing much damage. The ships did not reply, having orders to hold fire until the Prince of Hesse—who had landed with 1,800 men of the Marine Regiment east of La Linea—had summoned the town in the name of Charles III of Austria. To the summons the Spanish governor replied that as he held the town in the name of Philip V of Spain he and his men would defend it with their lives. Then began the long bombardment; the evacuation of women and children to Europa Point; the landing of the Marines between the fortress and the Point; and at last, after the Marines and a detachment of seamen had attacked from two sides, the capitulation. The garrison marched out with all the honours of war, and deservedly; for there were only 500 men and 100 guns to oppose the 14,000 men and 1,500 guns of Byng's detachment.

That stubborn resistance, vain though it was, afforded useful aid to the avenging fleet when it should arrive. When the French came out of Toulon to retake Gibraltar, as they must do or be held fast in the Mediterranean for the rest of the war, their powder-magazines and shot-lockers would be fully stocked; and they would meet an enemy whose irreplaceable reserves of ammunition were gone, used in the hours of ceaseless pounding that had breached the walls of impregnable Gibraltar.

II

Admiral Sir Clowdisley Shovell mounted the poop ladder of *Barfleur*, stiffly and with a certain amount of clanking, and acknowledged the doffed-hat salute of Captain Stuart. (It was an odd circumstance, all things considered, that his flag-captain should bear the name of James Stuart; but this Stuart's red face and fierce blue eyes were not at all like the sallow countenance of the one-time Lord High Admiral, now dead and buried.) The stiffness and noisiness of Sir Clowdisley's tread were due to the suit of black Spanish armour he was wearing, which clad him from neck to calf—breast-plate and back-plate, pauldrons and cuisses. His large bland periwigged countenance emerging at the top, and his silk stockings and buckled shoes at the bottom, might have looked incongruous to an antiquary, but the admiral cared nothing for incongruity; Rooke himself wore body-armour and half the captains in the fleet—Stuart was not one of them—took similar precautions against the enemy musket-men. Plate of proof could turn a musket-ball or a flying splinter. Since Sir Clowdisley's part in the coming battle was the Olympian one of issuing commands and remaining above the hurly-burly, he saw it as the behaviour of a fool to neglect his own protection.

The battle was very imminent. That was why he had donned the armour, which was damned uncomfortable for a portly gentleman of 54.

"Fifty-one Frenchmen, Sir Clowdisley, and a league and a half distant in my estimation." Captain Stuart was loquacious and given to stating the obvious. "Mark you the craft in rear of their line—galleys, a score at least. Otherwise, we're equal numbers so far as the line goes."

"Yes," said the admiral absently.

He had his glass to his eye, turning it slowly through a wide angle to scan the French fleet. The sunshine of the forenoon flashed from the white crests scurrying across the blue before a fresh easterly breeze, and the sails of the French battle-line, stretching for two miles along the western horizon, gleamed white as the plumage of swans, a vast convoy of which they something resembled.

"Equal numbers, as you say, Captain Stuart," he remarked. "But they've ten three-deckers more than we have."

It was not this fact, however, that had brought the frown to his brow and the steely glitter to his little grey eyes. Behind and beyond the long row of white specks a pale shaft rose like a giant arrowhead into the hazy blue sky. The Rock of Gibraltar; and the French were between it and the Anglo-Dutch fleet.

This situation, whereby the defending fleet found itself in the posture of attack, had come about by mischance. It had taken some time, as it was bound to do, for the news of the capture of Gibraltar to reach Toulon and for the Count of Toulouse to receive orders to sail and recapture it at all costs. Even so, when no news of the French had been received by August 9th, Rooke began to doubt their coming and sent a reconnoitring squadron to look for them. They were found quickly, and *Centurion* flying with the news brought all the fleet back with her—only to find that the French had vanished, presumably back to Toulon. In reality the ships that had been sighted were Toulouse's own reconnaissance squadron, and they had retreated eastward to rejoin and form with their main body. Rooke, who was not to know this, cast north and south across the Mediterranean in search of his enemy, who meanwhile—and while he was over the horizon towards the African coast—was making straight for Gibraltar with a following wind. With George of Hesse and a thousand Marines for garrison, Gibraltar was no prize for the French until they had dealt with the British who had now returned from a fruitless search to find them barring the way to the Rock. Toulouse must deal a crushing blow, win an overwhelming victory, before his country could again control the Mediterranean portals.

Sir Clowdisley, apparently imperturbable as he watched the blue plain of sea narrowing between the two fleets, was aware that this was no ordinary sea-fight. It was not a matter of sinking and taking ships and counting the score afterwards, but a battle for final possession of a valuable base. The English had to break through that barrier of ships and ranked guns, or hit it so hard that it could no longer stand against them. Either way the fighting would be fierce and long; and he knew too well that lack of powder and shot made a long fight a most perilous undertaking for Rooke's ships.

There was another thing that worried him. Here was a crisis in which fleet and squadron manœuvring might well turn the scale between fleets so evenly matched; and with the new signalling system for which he himself was largely responsible—flags of various colours hung in many positions and combinations—a flag officer could order his division to perform almost any evolution, even in the heat of battle. Yet this exercise of seamanship in the winning of battles was forbidden, including the "doubling" on the enemy which had saved Russell at Barfleur a dozen years ago. Rooke, with a shrug and a grimace, had shown him the explicit orders from their lordships which enjoined upon him the strictest adherence to Article XIX of their Fighting Instructions: *If the admiral and his fleet have the wind of the enemy, and they have stretched themselves in a line of battle, the van of the admiral's fleet is to steer with the van of the enemy's and there to engage them.* In short, both sides were to go on battering each other until one or both had had enough. That Rooke intended to comply with the order had been made plain half an hour ago when his ships had been brought into line abreast. Sir Clowdisley, who had been given command of the van, would have liked to see van, centre and rear sailing in line ahead to attack in three divisions, cutting the enemy line. It would have been risky, but not more so than the present method with its probable result of exhausting the English ammunition before a decision could be reached.

"Fore braces, there!" Stuart was shouting through his speaking-trumpet. "Slack away—handsomely—belay!"

The admiral looked to starboard, where *Namur* had fallen astern of the flagship. *Barfleur*, only six weeks out from England, had a cleaner bottom than most of Rooke's ships who had been at sea for more than six months, and tended to draw ahead of the line; Stuart was spilling some of his wind to regain station. *Namur*, he recalled, was commanded by Christopher Myngs, son of his old patron Sir Christopher. The remembrance took him on a sudden flight over thirty-eight past years, so that for a moment he was young Clow Shovell shivering at *Victory*'s masthead before the engagement of the Four Days' Battle. It could have been this mental flight that brought the physical reaction. The men of the Marine Regiment who were now tramping up to line the poop rail (a gaudy sight in their new red coats and white belts) stood aside at the admiral's curt order so that he could relieve himself into the scuppers; an operation not rendered easier by the folds of chain-mail with which the Toledo armourer had protected the opening in the front of his cuisses.

Beyond *Namur* lay the remaining thirteen ships of the line which with two sixth-raters and three fireships made up his division, the van. Beyond these again were the two dozen ships of the centre under Rooke, and the Dutch of the rear division commanded by Van Wassenaer. *Boyne* was five ships away from *Barfleur*, whose station was at the extreme southern end of the long line, and invisible from the poop-deck. How would James comport himself in the coming fight, Sir Clowdisley wondered; and experienced a stab of anxiety for his safety. Lord Dursley was no longer the beautiful boy who had so captivated him nine years ago but he had lost none of his attraction for the older man. Clow doubted uneasily that he was besotted on the lad.

"I shall go to the quarter-deck, Sir Clowdisley—we'll be into 'em in twenty minutes, in my estimation."

Stuart's voice recalled him to the present crisis. The French fleet was barely two miles away now, the long row of red and brown hulls seeming to reach from horizon to horizon. The northern end of their line, he reflected, must be within sight of Cape Malaga. They were all lying-to under topsails, ready to swing their broadsides; except—he noticed it that instant—the southern division, opposite the English van, who were making sail. No doubt about what they intended.

"Captain Stuart!" Stuart, half-way down the poop ladder, turned. "Signal the van 'Make sail to larboard.' And put this ship on a course sou'-west by west."

The captain, looking his astonishment, nevertheless roared the necessary orders through his speaking-trumpet. *Barfleur* bore ponderously away, altering course three points to larboard, and one by one the thirteen ships of the van brought the wind on their larboard quarters and drew away from the centre. By the time all were on the new course the enemy manœuvre Sir Clowdisley had anticipated was plain to see.

"Devil take me if they aren't trying to double on us!" said Stuart, eyeing the admiral with respect. "You've foxed 'em, though, sir."

"I trust so, sir," returned Sir Clowdisley mildly.

Evidently no autocratic Board had forbidden the French to try and get round on the rear of their enemy, and their van was attempting it, reaching far to the south-east in order to turn the end of the English line. That line, however, was now extending itself to block the attempt, and unless the French van chose to engage when the two converging divisions met, with a wide gap separating them from their main fleet, they must put about to close up again with their centre.

It was the widening gap between his own division and Rooke's ships that was Sir Clowdisley's chief anxiety now. But Sir George would have to look after himself—his manœuvre to check the "doubling" was a vital one and had to be carried out. A mile between the fleets—long gunshot. And there went the first broadside, from the centre astern of him. The reason, he saw at once, was that Toulouse had perceived the chance offered by that gap and had detached part of his centre to penetrate it. Close-hauled, the French ships were standing eastward; and Rooke was opposing the sally with broadsides at full elevation—hitting with them, too, for he saw a French topmast fall and a moment afterwards his glass showed him the spritsail yard of another ship trailing from her bowsprit.

"They're turning tail, Sir Clowdisley," Stuart announced gleefully. "And Sir George is signalling for close engagement. If I repeat the signal, and order course west by north——"

"Give those orders, if you please," said the Admiral shortly.

The ships of the French van were scurrying back across the white-flecked blue to re-form the line. As *Barfleur* and her sister ships turned to head straight for the enemy again, the abortive raid on the English gap ended and that French detachment, too, returned to take station in the rank of floating fortresses. The two parallel lines of warships, less accurately aligned but still in close battle formation, faced each other across the rapidly narrowing strip of sea, the one almost motionless, the other rushing towards it. After Rooke's two or three broadsides there had been no more firing, and as the few minutes necessary for coming within range passed the only sounds were the surge of water beneath the bows, the thrumming of the wind in the cordage, and the high-pitched shouts of the topmen taking in sail. Under reefed topsails the fifty-one great ships of the English fleet swung hard to a-larboard as they came within half musket-shot and the colossal uproar of the cannonade began. It was not to slacken for three hours.

Aloof by the taffrail at the highest part of *Barfleur*'s lofty poop, Sir Clowdisley was in the battle but not of it; or so he felt more than once. It was for Stuart and his dozen officers to fight the ship, and Stuart's attention was chiefly occupied by keeping his vessel where she could do most damage to her adversary, a three-decker whose poop, red-painted with gilded ornamentation, towered a dozen feet above *Barfleur*'s. Muskets on that high poop did terrible execution among the men of the Marine Regiment, and twice a bullet glancing off the Toledo armour reminded the Admiral that he was indeed in the battle though he was for the present hardly more than a spectator. But blood and wounds, the screams from a smashed gun-crew on the after-deck, the ear-splitting report that told of an upper spar shot away, were things of no great concern to him whose duty it was to wield as one weapon—should the chance come —a unit of thirteen ships each engaged like *Barfleur* in a life-and-death struggle. Between the drifting smoke-clouds he strove to obtain some idea of how the fight was going; it was well-nigh impossible. Only from the ceaseless thunder of the broadsides could he hazard a guess—it was little more—that there was neither yielding nor advantage on either side.

Minutes and hours crawled by and the gunfire roared on. The French were aiming high according to their usual custom and *Barfleur*'s rigging was a patternless network of dangling cordage. The main topsail yard, shot away and hanging by its slings, crashed against the mast each time the ship reeled to the discharge of the guns. The iron balls smashed into the heart-of-oak, the carving and gilding of a thousand craftsmen was hurled away in splinters, the shattered bodies were lugged below for the surgeon's saw and the pitch-pot, and still the guns thundered on. For the third time the admiral was hit, and saved by his armour. A 16-pounder ball ploughed a white groove across the deck, launching a flight of huge splinters, one of which smote Sir Clowdisley in the chest and hurled him to the deck. The blow drove the wind from his lungs, but he was no more than badly bruised. When he regained his feet he saw that the three-decker who had fought *Barfleur* so long was drifting away through the smoke, and the smoke itself was clearing. Moreover, there was a lessening of gunfire in his immediate vicinity, though he could hear no diminishing in the battle-thunder from the centre—far to northward—where Rooke was engaged with Toulouse's strongest division.

The thinning of the smoke, shredded away before the fitful south-easterly breeze, confirmed his hopes: the French van was drawing away from him, out of range. With ragged sails hoisted on splintered masts, their red sides blackened and torn, the great ships were pulling out of the fight. Not one of them had struck, all were still to be reckoned with, but they had received so terrible a pounding that they had to fall back for breathing space and to lick their wounds. Should he make sail, press forward and engage again? Steadying himself by the huge stern-lantern, he stood on the broad rail to glance keenly along his line northward.

Barfleur's hard pressing had taken her well out to the front of the battle-line and he had a clear and alarming view of the situation. Half a mile away the fierce action between the opposing centres was raging, a vast mound of smoke a-flicker with gun-flashes concealing all but a few half-revealed hulls and jutting masts. Standing back from it, well behind his own ragged line, were half a dozen English ships. He could recognize *Grafton*, *Monmouth* and *Nassau*—those three had taken part in the bombardment of Gibraltar and likely enough so had the others. He did not doubt that they had withdrawn for the simple reason that they had exhausted powder or shot or both. But their withdrawal from the line had left a mighty gap, three cable's-lengths at least, between *Yarmouth* on the flank of his own division and the nearest ship of Rooke's centre. Worse still, the weakness had been seen; for out of the smoke wreaths edged a French three-decker, shaking out her sails as she came, and after her another. Unless the gap could be closed, and swiftly, Rooke would be taken between two fires. And there was no time for the van to make sail, to put about.

"Captain Stuart!"

He had gone in three bounds to the head of the poop-ladder. The captain, hatless and with a bandage on one sleeveless arm, spun round at that enormous voice.

"Signal 'All ships back astern'. Blue and white flags at mizzen yard-arm. Instantly!"

Stuart, unaware of the danger, may well have wondered if Sir Clowdisley had gone out of his mind. But there was that in the Admiral's tone that precluded any question. Up sailed the flags with their unusual command, orders shrilled, men scurried aloft. *Barfleur*, with courses and topsails backed and straining queerly against her spars, began to move astern.

Sir Clowdisley was back at his post by the stern-lantern. *Barfleur* in her advanced position was in sight from *Yarmouth* at the other end of the line, and if Jasper Hicks had his wits about him he would see the flagship's signal and act at once. And it was so. *Yarmouth* backed her sails and was gathering sternway while the ships of Toulouse's wing were yet a quarter of a mile short of the fatal gap. It was still possible for the leading Frenchman to cross *Yarmouth*'s bows, though. Would she succeed?

Stuart's first lieutenant had come on the poop-deck to shout steering directions to the helmsmen below the spar-deck. It was very necessary. *Namur*, her bowsprit-end less than a pistol-shot from *Barfleur*'s stern, was yawing and making a poor show in this unfamiliar progress. But the fitful breeze was no longer from the south-east. It had veered westerly at a good time, and the waddling procession of ships quickened its stern-first pace until at last the thunder of *Yarmouth*'s broadside proclaimed that she had intercepted the enemy. The French spearhead was turned aside. But this time it was not withdrawn. One by one, as they drew sluggishly northward and closed the gap, the ships of the van engaged with new antagonists; and the smoke and din of the fight enveloped them once more . . .

"*The engagement lasted till about seven o'clock, when the enemy bore away and left us. Most of the masts and yards in the fleet were wounded to an irreparable degree.*" So wrote Admiral Sir George Rooke in his Journal. He did not add—perhaps because it was not ascertained until much later—that 782 officers and men of the Anglo-Dutch fleet were killed in the engagement, and 1,905 severely wounded.

Gibraltar was won, for centuries to come. But in the Battle of Malaga that won the Rock there was not a ship sunk or taken, nor had the sea-fight ended in a decisive victory for either fleet; which may have had some bearing on the reward meted out to the English admiral in command, though Sir Clowdisley always swore (with unusual fluency and vigour) that it was all owing to his damned meddling with politics. Something was owing, no doubt, to the date of Malaga, August 13th, which chanced to coincide with the date on which the Duke of Marlborough won his great victory of Blenheim. For the Tories, seeking some hero wherewith to counter the great Whig duke, claimed that Rooke's triumph was as great as that of Marlborough, upon which the Whigs (who had the advantage of being in the flood-tide of power) made it quite clear that Malaga was a useless, inconclusive sea-skirmish and George Rooke an incompetent who had failed to turn it into the victory it should have been. And Rooke, removed from his rank of Admiral of the Fleet, was never again employed in Britain's naval affairs.

III

Barfleur lay at anchor in Gibraltar Bay. Malaga was ten

days ago, and intensive labour had closed the holes in her sides, fished her shattered spars, and rove new sheets and halyards for the voyage home. All but a squadron of a dozen less badly wounded ships, under Vice-Admiral Sir John Leake, would sail next day for England.

Admiral Sir Clowdisley Shovell was at his table in the stern-cabin dealing with reports and letters. A deal of practice in correspondence with their lordships had brought more ease to his writing of late, and in view of the many and various ways his correspondents spelt not only his awkward surname but also his Christian name he had formed the habit of signing himself "Clow^d Shovell". The sunlight glittering on the water under the ship's stern windows sent discs and patines of gold to perform endless evolutions across the deck-beams overhead, and he sweated though he had loosened his neckcloth and taken off his wig.

A thunderous knocking sounded at the cabin door and the Marine soldier who was stationed there pushed it open. It was something new for Sir Clowdisley to have a soldier on guard at his cabin door and he rather liked it.

"Gennleman wishes to speak to ye, sir," said the Marine. "Captain o' the *Boyne*."

The admiral jumped hastily to his feet, clapped on his wig, tied his neckcloth.

"James, my dear lad!" He crossed to meet the newcomer with arms outstretched. "This is very well. I'd thought you too much occupied to visit me. That new foremast ——"

"The new foremast is stepped and rigged, sir. And since you're for home waters tomorrow, and I have a request to make, I made opportunity."

Lord Dursley was as splendidly handsome, as graceful, as careless of his charm, as ever. He was richly dressed in dark blue velvet, and the dancing lights from the water beyond the windows glinted on his gold-buckled shoes and on the big

167

emerald ring on his finger. The admiral's heart turned over as he looked at him.

"A request, James? It's granted before you make it." He went to a locker on the bulkhead. "Be seated—you'll take a glass of Madeira?"

"Thank you." Dursley took a chair at the table. "Yet I must tell you frankly that mine is no easy request."

Sir Clowdisley filled the two glasses and raised his own with a smile.

"I drink to the ninety-gun ship that may soon be yours," he said. "If Sir George has aught to say in the matter it will not long be delayed."

Dursley's answering smile was small and brief. He sipped at his wine and set it down.

"I fancy", he said slowly, "that Sir George Rooke's recommendations may not find favour with those in power. He is, after all, a Tory body and soul. It's on this account I come to you, sir."

"Indeed?" The admiral was puzzled. "I carry no weight in politics, James. That you have my goodwill you know——"

"And that is all I ask," said the young man quickly. "A letter. A recommendation from Admiral Sir Clowdisley Shovell. Nothing else is needed."

"Recommendation?" frowned Sir Clowdisley. "For what, may I ask, that your commanding admiral cannot give?"

Lord Dursley took a long drink of Madeira; one might have thought that his self-assurance was for once unequal to the present matter.

"You know, I think," he said carelessly, "that my family of Berkeley has very many branches, and that every branch is deeply concerned—and very powerful—in things that concern the government of England. The armed services, too. I may say, I hope, that I merit my post-captaincy?"

"None more so," Sir Clowdisley assured him eagerly. "Sir George's praise of your conduct at Malaga——"

"Yet", Dursley went on unheeding, "I would not hold it had I not been a Berkeley. I trust I'm not undeserving of a higher rank, and this also my birth would procure for me—you see I am frank—as it would also procure for you, sir, the rank you truly deserve. A moment"—he waved a slim hand gracefully as the older man made to interrupt—"let me ask if you have not, at some time, wished to name yourself Admiral of England?"

It was the vision Clow had kept in his secret heart all these years. A vision unlike to become reality save by some rare chance of political need.

"I—I——" he stammered.

"In no man that I know of," said Dursley, a charming smile revealing teeth like pearls, "would such a wish be more reasonable. And of course the Berkeley influence, like the good fairy in the tale, can make such wishes come true. But that is by the way. My own case is both simpler and not so simple. Berkeley or not—and if Nature takes her course I shall be Earl of Berkeley in a year or two—I can't achieve my own wish without your help. For I understand that a strong recommendation from a sea-officer of admiral's rank is essential for promotion to rear-admiral."

Sir Clowdisley spilled the wine that was half-way to his lips. He set the glass down slowly.

"To—rear-admiral?" he repeated incredulously.

"I told you when first we met, I fancy, that I was ambitious of advancement."

A boy of 24—rear-admiral. It was preposterous. It meant the passing over of a hundred experienced post-captains, mature men, deserving men, good seamen. It meant the very thing he condemned and fought against in his early years.

"A letter is a small thing, after all," said James, Lord Dursley; he was admiring the sparkle of reflected sunlight in the wine. "But so much can result from it—for us both."

Grey eyes under long dark lashes met Sir Clowdisley's

troubled gaze. They seemed to smile a little, with memory of past friendship.

"You'll do it, won't you, Clow?" he said softly.

Admiral of England, thought Clow. An earldom almost a certainty, and Elizabeth—dear, plump, loving Elizabeth—a countess. Narbrough had only been a knight.

"I'll do it, James—of course," he said quickly.

"And I knew you would, sir—of course." Dursley finished his wine and rose with hand outstretched. "I may not linger. But we shall meet again in England. Perhaps in London— perhaps at Court?"

"So that we meet," said Sir Clowdisley, "I care not where it is."

James laughed pleasantly, nodded, was turning away. He hesitated and then swung round with something in his hand.

"I venture to give you a keepsake," he said. "It's a family thing—call it a Berkeley pledge if you will. And now—God be with you, dear Clow."

He went out of the cabin, leaving his ring with its huge emerald in the admiral's grasp.

Sir Clowdisley sat for some moments with his gaze on the closed door of the cabin. After a while he sighed deeply, and looked at the ring in his hand as if he was seeing it for the first time. He slipped it on his finger, held it up to see the green glimmer deep in the jewel. It was the light from the restless sea that made it glow like a lamp.

EIGHT

The sweet tenor voice was young Trelawney's. His song came clearly down through the deck-head to the admiral's private cabin:

> *Over the mountains and under the waves*
> *Over the fountains and under the graves*
> *Over floods that are deepest*
> *Which Neptune obey*
> *Over rocks that are steepest*
> *Love will find out the way.*

There followed a muted clamour of applause and laughter and jest from the quarter-deck overhead. Young men's voices; and a young man's song. *Love will find out the way*—the admiral sighed, smiled, and shook his head. The small greyhound beside his chair stirred at the sigh and lifted his thin muzzle inquiringly, to be soothed by the caress of his master's hand.

A new and more distant music was sounding now: the shrill song of a fiddle—no, two fiddles. Men's voices took up the tune, too far away for the words to be audible. Sir Clowdisley sang them soundlessly to himself, for they had been familiar to him for half a century; the age-old ballad turned into a capstan-chanty, *To all you Maydens now on Shore*. The loud shouting of the deck officers and the drumming of bare feet on the planking above him drowned the chanty, and the timbers that made the walls of his cabin all creaked together suddenly as the anchor-cable hove taut. *Association* was about to weigh anchor. Very soon now she would turn her enormous gilded stern with its blazon of the royal arms towards the Rock, and once more it would be farewell to Gibraltar. She was going home.

In the Navy of Her Majesty Queen Anne there was no 100-gun ship so well-found, so lavishly equipped, or so splendidly furnished between-decks as *Association*. For so notable a person as an admiral of the fleet who was also a commander-in-chief—and, moreover, Rear-Admiral of England—this was only fitting. But Sir Clowdisley, finding the magnificence of his great cabin a trifle overpowering, had caused a small but comfortable cabin to be built into the upper stern gallery on the larboard side, and here—it was very clearly understood by all on board—he was to be left in peace, uninterrupted save in the most extreme emergency. He had found the place and its rigid rule invaluable during the past eleven months of uneasy co-operation with the Allied army under the Duke of Savoy in its attempt to capture Toulon. His refuge meant escape from the belabouring tongues of generals in disagreement, from bedlamite demands that the Navy should take its ships where there was not enough water for a cockboat. Only Mumper (he was named after James the Second's little dog) was *persona grata* here, and Mumper knew more about ships and seaways than did dukes and generals. That the Toulon expedition had failed was not the fault of the Navy. Sir Clowdisley's ships had made possible the passage of the Var and set the troops on their way for the abortive siege; and though the assault had been in vain, the Navy's part—an attack on the French fleet in harbour—had added a triumphant sequel to the Battle of Malaga by finally destroying the last threat to England's supremacy at sea. Ten great ships of France had been destroyed, and the French themselves had burnt the rest to prevent them from falling into enemy hands.

Association was swinging slowly; so her anchor was a-cockbill. Through the wavery glass of the window-panes he could see the white houses and grey-green scrub moving past a half-gunshot away, glowing gold in the October sun. The guns of the fort began their salute. He ought in courtesy to be on deck —but what was the use of being the high personage he was if he couldn't take his ease at any time he pleased? There were no less than two captains in *Association*, and Edmund Loades (he was Elizabeth's nephew) and his second Captain Whitaker were surely courtesy enough for the ceremony of leaving port. Sir Clowdisley, gently stroking Mumper's smooth head, frowned a little. Odd that he should be content to sit here below decks while his ship shook out her courses and gathered way towards the Strait. A few years ago he would have counted the man who could do such a thing a lubber. Maybe age had something to do with this diminishing of enthusiasm—or could it be that achievement had brought complacency and indolence in its train?

Not that achievement was yet complete. He was Rear-Admiral of England (of Great Britain now, he supposed, since the Union with Scotland last year) but there were still two steps to take before the final and highest honour. He took his hand from Mumper's head and touched the emerald ring on his finger; the dog gave the faintest of whimpers as he did so. Those two steps were nothing when he had the Berkeley family—apparently innumerable and everyone in a position of influence—pushing away behind him. Among the latest batch of letters from England had been an unofficial note from Sir Thomas Lyttelton at the Admiralty informing him that his recommendation of Lord Dursley would not only go forward but would also procure the young man's advancement to vice-admiral. "Love will find out the way?" In such matters as these Influence was the better pilot, thought Clow Shovell with a wry smile.

The regular thud and shudder of *Association*'s guns replying to Gibraltar's salute had accompanied his meditations. Now they were silent, and the big ship was heeling slightly to the southerly breeze as she drew away towards the narrows of the

Strait. Sixteen days to Spithead if the wind held fair; but October was a bad month to arrive off Ushant, and contrary gales could make the passage as long as three weeks. Still, nothing could prevent him from being at Courtlands for November 20th, his fifty-seventh birthday. He thought with pleasure of the wide hearth and the blazing logs, of Elizabeth and his two daughters sitting with him; and of course John and James Narbrough, though the lads were with him now, on board *Association* as supernumerary lieutenants.

The panes of the cabin window now held a picture of the open sea, dark blue under the fast sinking autumn sun. He got up and went to the window—Mumper instantly following— to press his cheek against the glass for a look astern. Three of the fourteen ships in company with *Association* could be seen —Lord Dursley's *St George* of 96 guns, *Royal Anne*, and *Romney*. Besides the fifteen of the line there were five fireships and a sixth-rate; a fleet of twenty-one vessels, leaving the Mediterranean to the command of Admiral Dilke and his squadron of thirteen. An English fleet wintering at Gibraltar, supreme in the Middle Sea! Rooke would be remembered as the man who gave the vital base to England, which was but just. All the same, young John Narbrough had been the real origin of the plan, not to mention its bringing forward by his stepfather, and it was right that these things should be placed on record— in the Memoirs of Admiral Sir Clowdisley Shovell, perhaps. That was a task for his leisure at Courtlands, and those memoirs should include praise of a Navy Secretary, Mr Samuel Pepys, whose work appeared to be totally forgotten already by those in authority. Or (the thought excited him) it might be well to wait a little, until they could be the Memoirs of Clowdisley Shovell, first Earl of Courtlands. He lost himself for a moment in consideration of that prospect. Courtlands was a trifle small as an earl's estate and residence, but it could be enlarged. He had the money to do it; especially with what he was bringing home.

Sir Clowdisley took a key from a pocket inside the waistband of his breeches and went—Mumper at his heels—to a sea-chest in one corner of the cabin. This he unlocked, revealing five smaller chests of dark Spanish oak bound with brass. A second key unlocked one of these and he stood with it open in his hands gazing at the contents—golden *ocho reales*, necklaces and gauds of jewels; they represented gifts from foreign notables and a ransom or two, some cunning bargaining on his own account, payment for extra services not covered by Her Majesty's commands. Clow Shovell of Cockthorpe was a wealthy man now. A great man. A nobleman to be. And beyond this there was still more to be achieved in preferment with the Berkeleys to aid him.

If he caught a glimpse, in the midst of so much gain, of something bright that was lost, it was too brief to prick his complacency.

He locked his treasure away and sat down again with Mumper at his knee. Yes—this homeward voyage would be a pleasant one indeed, in the good company of friends and family connections who yet acknowledged the respect due to his high rank. Edmund Loades, to be sure, showed some tendency to presume on his relationship to Lady Shovell; but Loades was a first-rate seaman, a qualification which would always excuse presumption in Sir Clowdisley's eyes. Then there was Sam Whitaker, best of good fellows, who had fought at Malaga and Gibraltar and had outrageous yarns to spin of his adventures in the West Indies. Henry Trelawney, son of the Bishop of Winchester, should make another at the admiral's table as company for John and James Narbrough. Trelawney's singing and James's flute should entertain them in the evenings, and when the weather permitted he would have the other James on board from *St George*, and Byng—Sir George Byng now— from *Royal Anne* to make up the party, and the cask of Mountaigne Allicant should be broached to set the merriment afloat. . . .

"Topmasts stays'ls, fore and main! Look alive there, you topmen!"

The cry from on deck roused him. He must have fallen into a doze. Stays'ls—they were out of the Strait, then, and setting course for Cape St Vincent 70 leagues west-nor'-west. North 150 leagues to Finisterre; across the Bay another 180; and so into soundings well to southward of those miles of reef and shoal off the Scillies. He had made the voyage so often that it was like walking up the south avenue to the door of Courtlands, a homecoming. Sir Clowdisley smiled a little at the thought, and then roused his big body from its half-recumbent position in the chair. Daylight was fading and soon his servants and stewards would be serving an evening meal in the great cabin. He would take the air on deck for a while first. He took his hat and cloak, ordered Mumper to his square of carpet behind the door, and went up to the quarter-deck.

The sinking sun was flooding sky and sea with a rich orange-coloured glow, painting *Association*'s piled clouds of canvas a gorgeous saffron. Astern and on either hand her consorts leaned sail-crowded masts before the steady southerly wind, a wind that for all its journey from the African deserts held an autumn coolness. On the flagship's quarter-deck the many-hued coats of a dozen officers were all tinged with the same orange glow, as though seen through a piece of coloured glass. The conversation among them fell abruptly to silence as the admiral appeared; which was as it should be.

Loades stepped forward to meet him. But before he could speak there came a hail from the masthead, clear and high as the cry of a gull.

"La-a-and ho! Broad on th' stabboard beam!"

"That will be Cape Trafalgar, Sir Clowdisley," said Captain Loades.

II

The twenty-one ships set sail from Gibraltar Bay on 19th

September 1707, bound for Spithead. On October 21st they came into soundings. On that same day the *Tartar*, frigate, sailed from Plymouth with special orders. Her captain was *"to look out for Sir Clo. Shovell and his squadron to give him an account how the land bears from him, and the better to enable him to give a just account thereof, he is to make the land once every day if he conveniently can: to continue till he meets Sir Clo. Shovell, hears he is passed by him, or till further orders."*

In the western approaches and in the Channel itself it had been the worst October weather since the Great Storm of 1703 when twelve of Her Majesty's ships and unnumbered merchant vessels had been lost with all hands. Day after day, week after week, the gales drove in from the Atlantic, raising giant waves to smash jetties and piers along the coast and hold the Cornish fishing fleets stormbound in their little harbours. Worst of all for the deep-sea vessels was the haze or fog of flying moisture that persisted without once lifting, reducing visibility to fifty fathoms' distance and making landfall or celestial observation totally impossible. And a good landfall was essential in approaching the Channel from the west, even when a shipmaster had been able to ascertain his latitude by the stars; for there was no method yet discovered for finding a ship's longitude by observation. Given ordinary conditions, an ocean mariner could precisely establish his north–south position, but for his east–west position he could only use dead-reckoning, the estimation of the distance run by casting the log. Ships of the same convoy had been known to differ as much as fifty leagues in their estimates by dead-reckoning. So to ensure a clear run easterly up the Channel a vessel had to make her landfall, either the cliffs of Ushant—but most captains gave that dangerous area a very wide berth—or St Agnes island or the Western Rocks of Scilly at the north of the Channel entrance. These circumstances, with the importance of the fleet now overdue at Spithead, were sufficient reason for *Tartar*'s mission.

The bad weather started as soon as the fleet began to cross

the Bay, with Cape Ortegal bearing south by east fifteen miles distant as their last landfall. "A very violent gale from the W.," was the log entry on October 5th, and the next three days were merely repetition of it. From the 9th to the 15th there was a comparatively easy period of strong winds and moderately high seas, but three days of "very hard gales, with great seas" succeeded as the storm-tossed ships struggled on under double-reefed topsails, beating always north-west to keep well clear of that terrible lee shore. In nearly three weeks of strife with the elements much damage had been done. All the great ships managed to get their topgallant-masts sent down, but not before *Monmouth*'s main topsail had been ripped from the yard and *Somerset*'s topgallant yards on both fore and main snapped in two like sticks of firewood. The seams of all the ships were working open and the pumps going continuously. *Association* suffered a serious blow when a furious gust laid her on her beam-ends for a minute and cracked the mainyard near the slings; only a fortunate recession of the gale enabled her crew to put a fish upon the yard with a spare topmast, and woold it so that the mainsail could be reset if necessary. In all this unyielding battle, with every man soaked to the skin all day and everything below decks either drenched or damp with salt water, there was precious little opportunity for the merry parties Sir Clowdisley had envisaged.

For seventeen days they had seen nothing of the land nor was there any hope of seeing it. The enormous waves came charging out of the west with rain and spray driving horizontally over their crests, and when the ships rose shuddering from the trough it was only to see that grey wall of rain and spray still hiding everything but the next oncoming wave. But *Association*'s log had been streamed and her speed conscientiously recorded every hour, and by dead-reckoning at four in the afternoon of October 21st it was calculated that the fleet was in latitude 49° 30′ north. A cast of the lead confirmed that they were already in soundings. Sir Clowdisley, who had now taken over command, signalled all ships to heave to.

In such visibility obedience to this order depended on those ships who could see the signal flag carrying it out, and the others perceiving the repeated signal or imitating their neighbours. Fortunately the weather had chosen this hour to change, though not much for the better. The wind backed through sou'-west to sou'-sou'-west—a fair wind up-Channel—and the fierce drive of the gale became a strong wind strengthening in intermittent gusts to its former force, while the thick rain gave place to a haze in which neighbouring ships could be seen if they were within a cable's-length. Even so, the admiral's next signal—all ships to take soundings, all sailing-masters to come aboard flagship—took an hour to become effective; so that it was through the gloom of early evening that the boats came swooping on the green Atlantic rollers and the sailing-masters in turn made that desperate neck-or-nothing jump for the ladder.

The admiral received them in the great cabin. Its furnishings were far from magnificent now. Every fitting and ornament had been lashed in a tight mass and lashed again to the bulkhead, except for a single chair at the fixed table in the centre. The Turkey carpet was gone and the deck where it had been glistened with damp. Two of the stern windows had been smashed in and had boards nailed across them. Sir Clowdisley, his big round face calm and expressionless as it always was in emergency, sat in the chair with Captain Loades standing beside him and Mumper leaning a shuddering body against his shins. The men who stood round him swayed all together, far to one side and then to the other, as *Association* dived and climbed over trough and crest of the waves.

"Well, gentlemen, let's have your soundings," said the admiral. "If you're to rejoin your ships before dark we've little time enough. *St George*?"

"Eighty-five fathom, Sir Clowdisley," said Lord Dursley's

sailing-master. "Small black sand was all there was on the tallow. And I'll maintain you won't find small black sand in eighty-five fathom except in one place, and from that place the Lizard bears east-nor'-east a quarter north, and distant sixty-four leagues, so that——"

"God's life, man, you're a good fifty leagues out!" The interruption came from the sailing-master of *Lennox*, a fiery little man whose stubble beard showed red in the light of the swinging lantern. "We've been set far to north'ard of that. As for black sand, there's patches from here to the Smalls."

He was going on, but the admiral's uplifted hand stopped him. "I asked for your soundings, not for your opinions. *Monmouth*?"

"Sixty fathoms, sir—fine white sand."

"*Swiftsure*?"

"Sixty-five, sir—brainy sand with stones like beans."

Cruizer, too, had found brainy sand, but at fifty-three fathoms and with pieces of red mashed shells. *Panther* had brought up white sand, *Torbay* had found a rocky bottom. The others were as diverse in their findings. Sir Clowdisley heard them out and sat silent for a moment, reflecting. He could not tell what this variation in depth and bottom meant, but it was not impossible that such variations should exist under an area of three square miles of sea, which was roughly the area occupied by his ships as they lay hove-to. He turned to the most experienced sailing-master present.

"*Torbay*, what's our position by your dead-reckoning?"

"Latitude forty-nine degrees thirty minutes, sir."

"The same as our own finding, Sir Clowdisley," remarked Captain Loades with satisfaction. "By your leave, we're precisely where we should be—a good twenty leagues south of the Scillies, with the fairway before us and a fair wind for home."

There was a murmur of agreement from the assembled masters, but *Lennox*'s sailing-master did not join it. He was watching the admiral's face, ready to uphold his own convictions if he was given the chance. But Sir Clowdisley's abstracted gaze did not rest on him as it ran quickly over the brown faces confronting him.

"We may take it that we are at least ten leagues south of Scilly," he said slowly, "about the sixty-fathom line, and clear of the shoals—since only *Torbay* found rock. You'll return to your ships, taking my compliments to your captains and the orders I now give you to deliver. Make sail conformable to the weather and stand away in company, course east by north. That's all, gentlemen, until we meet in Spithead."

They went down the side one by one, as their boats came in soaring and falling on the monstrous waves, expertly judging the moment for the leap that wrongly judged meant almost certain death. It would take them some time to regain their ships, and further time would be needed for the hoisting-in of the boats, a ticklish job in a sea like this. The admiral, who had come on deck wrapped in his cloak, ducked under a shower of spray and turned to Captain Loades as the last boat drew safely away from the flagship's side.

"Square away when you see *Eagle* and *Romney* make sail, Captain. They'll be half an hour yet. Meanwhile, have the stern-lanterns lit."

It was nearing twilight. Out of the grey obscurity to westward rolled the endless ranks of the waves; a succession of marching mountain-ridges, colourless now, dark and menacing against the paler darkness of the haze. The admiral braced himself in the angle of the poop rail to await the moment of sailing. Under him the deck tossed itself skyward, tilted, dropped, rose again, to the accompaniment of a ceaseless chorus from every timber and shroud and spar on board—a shrieking and groaning that might have been the voices of wretched souls in Purgatory. The three big lanterns rocked and flickered above his head. A sudden great gust blew out two of them, but within the minute a seaman came aft with a flaring torch to relight them. The wind was rising again. That gust was fiercer than any in the past hour.

It was darkening fast. Dark enough now for him to perceive the dim glow from the binnacle, where the two helmsmen at the wheel below the spar-deck steadied her against the thrust and swing of the seas. So dark that the towering shapes of *Romney* and *Eagle* were barely discernible, their masts swinging wildly and their hulls vanishing and reappearing as the seas swept under them. But a strip of pale grey twitched and spread from *Romney*'s mainyard, and half a minute later the main courses appeared above *Eagle*'s tossing hull.

With the course he had ordered this would be a quartering wind, and a pair of low sails was the rig for this night's passage. Loades, a good seaman, would know that. Even as he gazed, a trifle anxiously, at the huge column of the mainmast the sail flapped and crackled from its brailings and was hauled taut. A shout from the quarter-deck, hurled into fragments by the wind, reached his ear.

"Meet her . . . steady . . . east by north . . ."

Association's stern lifted as she turned before the wind. Sir Clowdisley strained his gaze into the obscurity astern and made out five ships under way. Suddenly he was exceedingly tired; there had been no sleep for him in the past two days. He clambered down the poop ladder to the quarter-deck and found Loades and six or seven others there.

"I am going below, Captain. Pray call me if there's any change in wind or weather."

The cot in his private cabin had been wedged and lashed, and the blankets received him fully dressed. Mumper was there to thrust himself into the angle behind his knees as he always did. *The fairway before us and a fair wind for home*, thought the admiral; and on that thought fell asleep.

The great ships sailed on before the freshening gale, into the haze and the spindrift and the swiftly falling night. They sailed in the stations they had taken when they brought-to for sound-

ing, *Eagle* and *Romney* to larboard of the flagship and the rest
farther away on her starboard beam. And by that chance
Eagle and *Romney*, too, were doomed.

The shock hurled the admiral from his cot in to the corner of
the cabin. The blankets deadened the impact of his heavy body
on the locked sea-chest, but his head drove against the bulkhead and he lay momentarily stunned. His returning senses
brought a confused uproar to his half apprehension—a surging
thunder, a babel of shouting, Mumper's agonized yelps close
at hand. The planking under him shuddered horribly and
tilted still farther towards the cabin window, and from where
the window had been came a mighty gush of water to soak his
clothes and slop across his face. It was pitch dark.

She's struck. He had struggled to his feet before the full certainty of it thrust into his mind like a sword. *What of his other
ships?* That care, instant and automatic, was shortlived. The
blow of a giant hammer smote the shell of timber in which he
staggered and splashed, tipping it at a steeper angle and sending the water that lapped his ankles dashing against the lower
bulkhead to fly back at him in a shower of salt spray. Simultaneously there came from overhead a report like the explosion
of a 32-pounder, followed by a tremendous crash that shook
the wooden fabric of the ship. *Mainmast gone.* After the crash
the shrill cacophony of the storm seemed intensified. Mingled
with it were human screams and isolated yells. Then nearer
voices calling urgently.

"Sir Clowdisley! Sir Clowdis-*lee*!"

"Father! Are you——" A second crash overbore James's
cry; the pounding of the seas allowed him to hear a disjointed
message. "On deck . . . she's going . . . boat——"

"I come!" he roared against the tumult. "Look to yourself!"

The shock and confusion in his mind had gone, leaving it

cold, alert, swift-moving. How much time? But the key was already in his hand. He knelt with the sea-water lapping his thighs and flung open the chest. He could carry only one box, for here was Mumper whining and splashing beside him in the dark. The small heavy chest would go under one arm and Mumper under the other. As he stood up another hammer-blow and lurch sent him reeling against the cabin door. It flew open, precipitating him into the alleyway to bring up with a thump against an opposing bulkhead. The alleyway had taken on a steep slant downwards to the right, and the steps of the companion-ladder leading to the deck were almost level, so that instead of climbing he trod catlike on the edges of the treads, groping with his feet for the invisible foot-holds.

Clutching his treasure-chest and his dog, the admiral set foot on the roof-top slope of the quarter-deck and there halted as if petrified.

It was not black darkness here. A ghastly light, pallid and shifting, came from the haze of blown spray overhead and the white crests that lifted into it—lifted, hung toppling, crashed down in a mad swirl of foaming water that swallowed the whole larboard side of the deck as far as the stump of the main-mast. In that surging, roaring flood dark objects leaped and were sucked down again: broken spars, casks, the bodies of men. Above it the remnants of the mizzen rigging streamed horizontally in the screaming wind like thin stiff fingers, pointing for'ard, seeming to direct the onrush of the triumphant sea to where a confused mass of men strove to free the longboat from a tangle of cordage and spar. *Association*'s wounded hull lifted sluggishly as if she made a last despairing effort, then subsided with a frightful grinding. A gigantic wave smashed down with a noise like a thunderclap and raced for'ard to engulf the men at the longboat. Spume and spray from its upward surge lashed at the admiral where he crouched against the quarter-deck rail.

184

A hand on his arm. A voice yelling in his ear.

"The pinnace—we've got her away. Come on, sir!"

It was James Narbrough. He kept his grasp on his step-father's arm as they crept along the scuppers for a few paces, in the angle between the rail and the sloping deck. Knotted ropes had been made fast and hung overside. Below the black rim of the rail the ship's bulging side gave a lee where the steep hills of water charged past unbroken by the wind. The pinnace swooped and fell there while two pairs of oars flailed desperately to hold her in place. Again came the crash of a big sea on *Association*'s other flank, again the horrid grinding shook her like the throe of death.

"She's breaking up, sir—over with you, quick!"

The admiral took Mumper in one big hand, poised, judged, tossed the dog outboard. He saw the small black shape land in the boat and heard a yelp. Poor Mumper! But he had yet a chance, with a very few others. The little treasure-chest still under his left arm, he swung himself to the rail and grasped the knotted rope with his right hand. Feet and legs clasped the fall of the rope expertly. The muscles of his right arm cracked as he slid the clinging hand, writhing his fingers over the knots.

"Jump!"

The pinnace came heaving up under him. He flung himself clear, dropped, fell heavily and painfully between the thwarts. James came down upon him as he tried to rise and there was a moment of splashing and confusion—for the boat was half full of water—before he could glance about him. The black loom of the ship's side fell back. They had pulled clear. There was a chance of life. If they were among the Scilly shoals the islands were close at hand.

"Who is here?" he demanded.

John Narbrough's voice answered, breathless as he tugged at his oar. "Captain Loades, Trelawney, three seamen, James and myself. With you, eight of us."

And Mumper. The admiral twisted himself about to grope for the little greyhound. And he saw the great wave rising, soaring, towering above their stern. His cry of warning was stifled in its all-engulfing fall.

He was not below the surface for more than a few seconds. When his head came into the windy air and he could spit the salt from his mouth it seemed that he was quite alone. There was no boat, no ship, no one in the dark world of heaving water but himself. Without consciously directing his limbs he began to swim, rising and sinking on the huge mounds of the sea that swept him onwards willy-nilly to their own destination. That destination must be a coast, a shore. Hope and fear rose sharply, intermingled. It could be a shore of sand where these monstrous waves would break at last, casting him up with the chance of life; or it could be the razor-edged rocks of reef or cliff that would receive his hurtling body, to slash and mangle the life from him. There was no shaping his course now. His life was in the great hand of the sea.

He swam on, increasingly aware of the clogging weight of his clothing. Time left him gradually, freeing his spirit. The great ships, the battles, Elizabeth, King James, poor Mumper —these moved through his mind in company with Dick Parr and Mr Pepys and Juanita at Cadiz. Moved and shrank and faded. The man who was to be Admiral of England shrank and faded too. He was Captain Shovell of the *James* swimming a race with Matt Aylmer in the milk-warm Mediterranean waters; he was Clow Shovell, ship's boy, striking out for the *Arabella* with an urgent order from Sir Christopher Myngs; he was little Clow splashing joyously in the shallows on a holiday outing to Cley-next-the-Sea. And then all was gone. He was nothing. Until the physical shock and the thunderous roar called back a little of Clow Shovell to the big limp body lying in the surf, enough for the instinctive effort that drew him clear of the backwash of the waves, away from the clutch of the ebb-tide.

Once, and once only, the senses recalled again the fleeting spirit. There was a shifting, a touch on the finger that wore an emerald ring, a feeble struggle. It was very brief, and after it there was nothing more.

EPILOGUE

Extract from the *Dictionary of National Biography*,
Volume XVIII, page 161

. . . The body of Shovell, still living, was thrown on shore in Porthellick Cove, but a woman, who was the first to find it, coveting an emerald ring on one of the fingers, extinguished the flickering life. Near thirty years after, on her death-bed, the woman confessed the crime and delivered up to the clergy-man the ring, which thus came into the possession of Shovell's old friend, the Earl of Berkeley, to one of whose descendants it now belongs.

The body . . . was buried, at the cost of the government, in Westminster Abbey, where an elaborate monument in very questionable taste was erected to Shovell's memory.